Clint Did Not Seem Reasonable

Bob wasn't too worried about the clean-cut guy, Jim. Jim seemed reasonable, and he'd wandered off, looking through Bob's considerable collection of merchandise. Bob was worried about the dude with the mustache and the bad teeth, Clint. Clint did not seem reasonable. In fact, Bob was pretty sure Clint was a psychopath.

Clint was standing behind Bob, asking questions about Bob's customers. Bob wasn't eager to answer these questions—his customers trusted him, trusted that he was discreet, and if he betrayed that trust, those customers would take their business elsewhere. But Clint had just cut off the ring finger of Bob's left hand with a straight razor. Bob considered himself a pretty tough hombre, but he knew he wasn't tough enough to give up many more fingers. And what if Clint decided to use that razor to cut Bob's throat? The trust of his customers wouldn't be worth much to a dead Trader Bob.

"So you gonna tell me about the bitch and the Chief and his powerhouse?" Clint asked in that molasses southern drawl of his. "Or am I gonna cut off another one of your fingers?"

FOR A FEW ZOMBIES MORE

by Chance Shirley

based on the screenplay by
Chuck Hartsell and Chance Shirley

and the screen story by
Chuck Hartsell, Michael Shelton,
and Chance Shirley

A CREWLESS BOOK

Published by
Crewless Books
2717 Highland Ave S
Birmingham, Alabama 35205

This work is based on the screenplay by
Chuck Hartsell and Chance Shirley
and the screen story by Chuck Hartsell,
Michael Shelton, and Chance Shirley

Cover painting by Sonia J. Summers

Consulting editor: Andrew Bellware

ISBN: 978-0-9979810-0-1

Typeset in the United States of America
Second printing–January 2019

CONTENTS

FOR A FEW ZOMBIES MORE

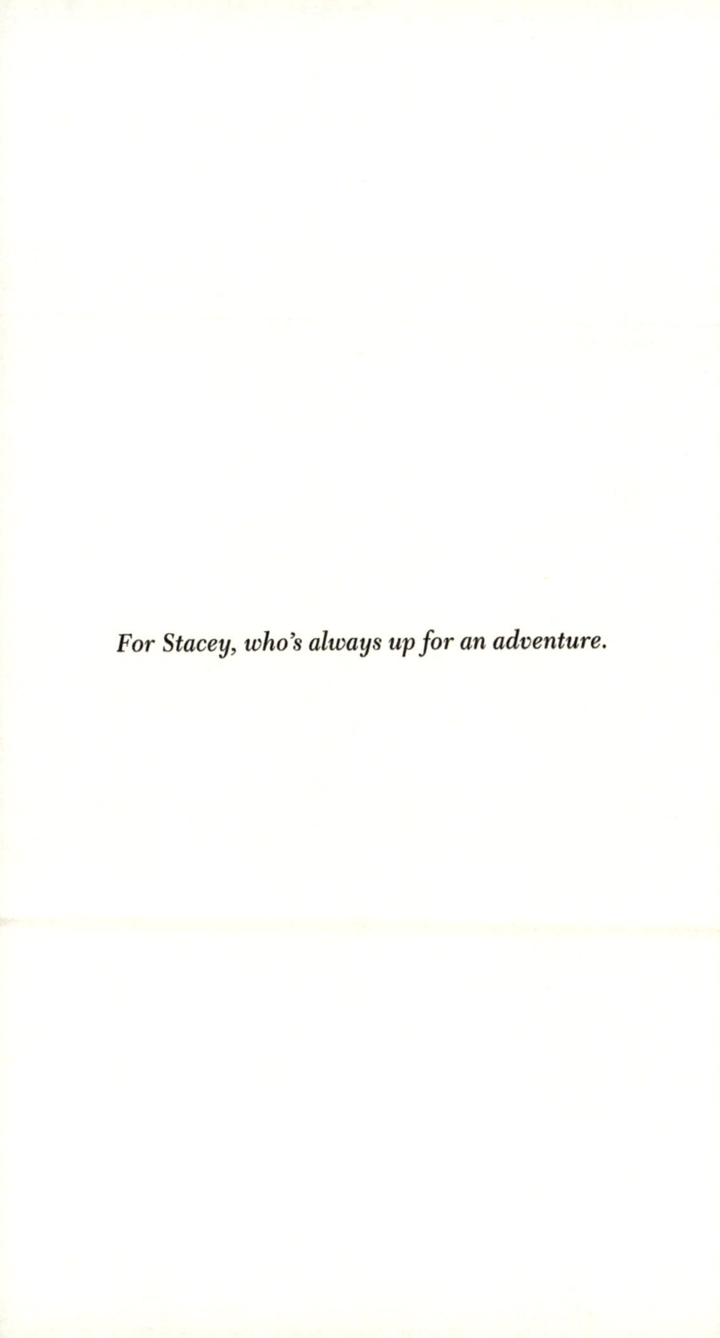

For Stacey, who's always up for an adventure.

Chapter 1

North of Thorsby

Chuck stopped his horse across the broken-up road from the old gas station. He reached beneath his poncho, drew his .44 revolver from its holster, and aimed it at the zombie that was shambling past just on the other side of the gas pumps. Each of the rusted pumps was marked with a faded red Texaco star.

If he hadn't seen the zombie, Chuck would have smelled it. After spending a decade in the occasional company of walking corpses, the odor of rotting meat still made his stomach turn.

The zombie stopped for no apparent reason, then slowly turned its head toward Chuck and stared at him—or maybe past him—with milky-white eyes. Chuck pulled back the hammer on his pistol until it stopped with a satisfying click, but he was in no hurry to start shooting.

Chuck noticed the Diet Mountain Dew bottle hanging from a length of rope tied to the zombie's neck but didn't give it much thought. Zombies were always getting tangled up in some stupid shit or the other. Back during the summer, Chuck had made an easy escape from a zombie struggling to chase him with a clothes-line and a couple loads of laundry tied to its right ankle.

Some sliver of intelligence in the zombie's rotting brain alerted it to the potential danger of Chuck's .44. Or maybe it saw something shiny in its peripheral. Either way, the zombie resumed its staggering. Chuck waited until it made it a safe distance away, then he carefully lowered the hammer on his pistol and holstered it.

"Let's go, boy," Chuck told his horse. He gave it a gentle nudge with the heels of his hiking boots, and the horse trotted across the road. Chuck dismounted, tied the horse's reins to one of the gas pumps, and grabbed the rifle that was strapped to the saddle.

Chuck saw the FOR SALE BY OWNER sign in the storefront window and wondered if some delusional bastard had tried to sell commercial real estate after the dead started rising from their graves and civilization went to hell in a handbasket. Or maybe the place was for sale before the shit hit the fan.

Based on the broken lock and missing doorknob, Chuck figured he wasn't the first person to ignore the NO TRESSPASSING sign nailed to the front door. He carefully pulled on the door. It opened with a creak. Chuck looked inside, smelled the air . . . more rotting meat. He pulled his bandana over his nose and mouth—bandit-style—and slowly walked into the gas station.

Chuck stepped over the broken cash register on the floor, ignoring the coins and the small bills—a couple hundred dollars worth—scattered around it. He walked past shelves long ago looted of their bags of chips and candy bars. He reached the cooler section, empty except for a single carton of Barber's milk. He read the expiration date: November 25, 2004.

Wait. There was one more thing in the cooler. A bottle of Budweiser on a high shelf. Chuck smiled. Was it possible every other looter had missed the bottle of beer? He reached for the bottle and frowned as soon as he lifted it. Empty.

A hand crept out between two of the lower cooler shelves and grabbed Chuck's leg. A zombie. Chuck dropped the Bud bottle. As it hit the floor and shattered, Chuck struck at the zombie's hand with the butt of his rifle. After a couple of blows, Chuck worked his way free from the zombie's grasp and staggered back a few steps.

And walked into another zombie.

Chuck turned to face the new threat. He swung his rifle like a bat, but the zombie was stronger than expected. The zombie caught the rifle and worked to take it away from Chuck as it tried to bite at his face with black and bloody teeth.

The rotting smell was overwhelming. Chuck thought about maybe replacing his bandana with a gas mask. He looked into the zombie's dead, milky-white eyes and wondered if these poor, disgusting ghouls could even see. Chuck's wandering mind was refocused on the fight when the zombie slammed him against an empty shelf. Chuck pushed back, pivoted, and let go of the rifle. Momentum carried the rifle, along with the zombie holding it, into the men's restroom. Chuck slammed the restroom door and leaned against it.

"Great," Chuck mumbled to himself. "A zombie has my rifle."

Chuck looked back to the cooler. The zombie was slowly crawling between the shelves. In a couple minutes it'd be free, and Chuck would have another fight on his hands. Chuck drew his pistol as he made a beeline for the cooler. He reached the cooler and pistol-whipped the zombie's hands and wrists until it retreated.

Chuck heard a noise behind him and spun to face it. *Knock. Scrape. Knock.*

It sounded like the zombie was trying to exit the bathroom but couldn't quite figure out the door. Chuck aimed his pistol at the bathroom door.

*Knock. Scrape. **BOOM.***

Chuck jumped back with a start as his rifle went off inside the bathroom. He waited. Listened. Nothing.

Waited some more. Listened again. Nothing.

Chuck slowly approached the bathroom. He put his ear to the door, listened for a third time. Still nothing.

A thick plume of gun smoke rolled out when Chuck finally opened the bathroom door. He looked inside to see the zombie sitting on the toilet, Chuck's rifle in its lap. The zombie's head had been almost completely blown away by the rifle shot. Its brains, blood, and several small pieces of its skull now covered the walls of the small room.

Chuck ran back to the gas station's front door and checked outside. Apparently, the noise of the brawl and rifle shot hadn't attracted any unwanted attention. His horse looked at him for a moment, then went back to munching on the blades of grass growing through the cracks in the concrete.

Chuck returned to the bathroom for his rifle. He wiped the rifle's barrel against the zombie's tattered shirt and got most of the blood and goo off it. He made one more pass around the shelves on his way back to the door when he saw them: a half dozen or so VHS tapes. And a DVD.

Chuck grabbed the DVD first, examined the cardboard and plastic case. *Goodfellas.* Great movie. But fairly primitive as far as DVDs go. Two-sided, so you'd have to get up halfway through the movie to turn over the disc, and non-anamorphic, so the resolution wasn't the best. But it was LaserDisc quality, give or take, and it was letterboxed to the original theatrical aspect ratio.

Back outside the gas station, Chuck put the VHS tapes and *Goodfellas* DVD in one of his saddlebags. He retrieved a hand-drawn map and pencil from his jeans pocket. After years of scavenging, all of the dollar stores, grocery stores, gas stations, and convenience stores had started to look the same, so Chuck had drawn a map of all the locations in the area where he might come across a DVD or videotape. He found the gas station on the map and marked it with an X.

Chuck secured his rifle, untied and mounted his horse, and made his way farther down the broken-up road. He had the feeling he was moving in the wrong direction. Then he saw the roadside sign and knew for sure. Through the dirt and rust and dead vines he could make out its message:

THORSBY: 3 MILES

"Whoa, boy," Chuck told his horse as he pulled on the reins. "Not that way."

The horse trotted a wide U-turn, then began walking north, away from the sign and away from the town of Thorsby, Alabama.

Chapter 2

Zombie Walk

The voice on the radio was singing about being left to its own devices. And something about a man being turned into a monkey. Iceman couldn't say for sure, he wasn't paying much attention to the lyrics. But he liked the beat and the sound of the guitars, and anything was better than just listening to the rumble of the Ford F-150 pickup truck's diesel engine.

Even though life in Alabama in the year of our Lord 2014 was mostly post-apocalyptic, it was nice that a few of the comforts of civilized life were still available, things like FM radio. The truck's radio was currently tuned to 94.7 FM, the on-air home of a guy who called himself "DJ Dan." Unlike the disk jockeys of old, Dan didn't have much of a speaking voice. But he had a pretty big collection of music and some serious broadcasting power—Iceman could pick up Dan's signal pretty much anywhere in central Alabama.

Tonight Iceman was driving to pick up . . . well, he wasn't exactly sure. Didn't care either. All he knew was he was driving north from Thorsby to Tarrant City to pick up something, and whatever it was would fit in the bed of the truck.

Clutch was currently snoozing in the truck's passenger seat. Not surprising as these truck runs tended to happen in the middle of the damn night. But Clutch would drive the truck on the return trip, as he always did, and then it would be Iceman's turn to nap. In the meantime, Iceman had the rock and roll music to keep him awake. That and the crystal meth.

The truck swerved a bit as Iceman felt around in his front shirt pocket and found his glass pipe and Bic butane lighter. He fired up the pipe, inhaled deeply, and immediately felt more awake. Hot damn this was good crank. That was one of the big perks of working for the Chief, the good crank.

Iceman cracked the window and exhaled the meth smoke. No sense stinking up the cab of the truck. It was smelly enough to begin with. A little cool night air would be another factor to help keep Iceman awake, and it wouldn't bother Clutch. That son of a bitch could sleep through anything.

Somewhere up the road a mile or two, a zombie staggered out of the woods at the road's edge. It tried to cross the road but something held it back—a length of rope around the zombie's neck was snagged on a low tree branch. The zombie was too dumb to realize what was happening, but it kept trying to walk until the branch bent, then snapped. The zombie took a few steps and had made it to the middle of the road when something got its attention—a light in the distance, getting brighter.

Like all zombies, this one had a fascination with light, especially electric light. The zombie started walking right down the middle of the road toward the fast-approaching light. Like all zombies, this one hadn't had much of a reason for walking wherever it was walking before it noticed the light, so this new course was as good as any.

The truck rounded a curve and Iceman could see the zombie in the middle of the road, shambling in his direction. Iceman turned the wheel slightly so the truck was driving down the middle of the road. He stepped on the accelerator.

The Ford F-150 pickup truck hit the zombie. *Clunk*.

Clutch woke with a gasp. He looked forward to see the zombie's ugly face pressed against the glass of the truck's windshield.

"Shit, man," Clutch said. "You run over somebody?"

The glow of Iceman's butane lighter illuminated his face as he took another hit from his pipe. "Zombie," he said.

The zombie stared at Clutch with empty eyes. The rope around the zombie's neck was attached to a plastic Diet Mountain Dew bottle. The bottle bounced against the windshield in the wind. "Oh," Clutch said. "So you ran over a nobody."

Clutch yawned, rubbed his eyes. He looked at the time on the truck's radio. No sense trying to get back to sleep now. They'd be in Tarrant City in fifteen minutes. He looked over at Iceman, pointed at the glass pipe. "Let me get some of that."

Iceman handed Clutch the pipe and lighter. Clutch fired it up and took a couple of hits. "Crack your window, man," Iceman said. Clutch complied, then sparked the pipe again.

The truck rolled into a sharp curve. There had been a guard rail at the road's edge, but it had fallen into disrepair years ago. Iceman whipped the wheel, and the zombie lost its feeble grip on the windshield wiper. It hit the road with a thud, rolled off the road and past where the guard rail had been, then tumbled down a hill and into the woods.

Clutch gave the pipe and lighter back to Iceman and the truck continued on toward Tarrant City.

* * *

At the bottom of the roadside hill, the zombie lay

still for a half hour or so, eyes closed, Diet Mountain Dew bottle still hanging from its neck. If anyone had walked past, they would have mistaken it for a regular old corpse, not one of the walking variety. But no one walked past, at least not for a half hour or so. Then the zombie's eyes popped open, and it slowly got back on its feet and started walking away from the road and the hill.

A couple hours of shambling and staggering later, the woods began to clear, and the zombie walked onto the asphalt of a parking lot somewhere at the edge of a city. The parking lot was empty except for a top-of-the-line 2003 model Honda Accord that was in pretty good shape except for all the blood on the upholstery and the corpse in the passenger seat. The zombie ignored the car and the corpse and continued its journey wherever it was going, which was almost certainly nowhere in particular.

* * *

This trio of zombies didn't smell any better than the last three. On the bright side, they probably didn't smell any worse than the next three would smell. It was slow work, moving a bunch of the shambling undead bastards from the bus to the warehouse, but if you tried to take more than three at a time, they'd more often than not end up in a pile on top of each other, making that weird moaning/wheezing/growling sound and pathetically writhing around. Herding cats would have been preferable.

Larry wasn't sure why they didn't park the bus closer to the warehouse door. And he wasn't really sure why they needed so many damn zombies. He and his compatriots were known for dining on the brains of the undead, but that was more for show, not their actual primary food source. There were rumors of scientific study, but Larry didn't know anybody smart enough to be a scientist. Most folks he knew weren't much bright-er than the zombies he was currently nudging toward the warehouse door.

At least catching the zombies was easy. A couple hours after sunset, Larry and Clint would drive around what was left of the city of Birmingham and the sur-rounding suburbs in a bus. It was one of those old yel-low school buses with the folding side door up front and the emergency exit dead center of the back. They'd ripped out most of the bus' little benches at this point and installed some of that metal mesh fencing so the passenger area of the bus was a big cage.

Whenever Larry or Clint spotted a zombie, they'd stop the bus and turn on a bright-ass spotlight they'd bolted onto the back of the bus. The zombie would make a beeline for that light—well, whatever passed for a beeline for a zombie. When the zombie got close to the bus, Larry would bind its hands with a big zip tie and throw a thick canvas bag over its head. The zombies didn't like that, especially the bag. Something about being in total darkness like that agitated the zombies. But it kept Larry safe from the ghouls' nasty and potentially deadly teeth, so he didn't give a shit about the zombies' opinion on the matter.

Larry had almost wrangled this group of zombies to the warehouse door when he saw something out of the corner of his eye. He turned his head to get a better look. On the sidewalk on the other side of the street there was another zombie, slowly making its way south. Larry didn't pay any attention to the Diet Mountain Dew bottle hanging from the thing's neck by a dirty length of rope.

"Looks like we missed one," Larry said.

Clint was a few steps behind Larry and the three bound and hooded zombies. He stopped to look across the street. He grinned, showing his dirty teeth—Larry figured some of these zombies probably had cleaner teeth than Clint—beneath his handlebar moustache.

"Always another zombie," Clint said.

Some people would have called Clint a psychopath. Larry would not necessarily have disagreed with that opinion. But whenever Clint talked, he didn't really sound like a high-ranking member of some post-apocalyptic gang. He sounded more like a genteel Mississippi lawyer in a tweed suit in one of those movies adapted from a John Grisham book where everybody drinks iced tea and sweats all the time because they don't have any air conditioning, even though they're in Mississippi.

Larry returned his attention to the task at hand and managed to move the three zombies a little closer to the warehouse door.

❋ ❋ ❋

The climb to the top of the building was not an easy one. Which was the point. Lee had carefully searched the building's interior earlier. He'd found two zombies—one large, one extra large, both quickly dispatched with a knife to the forehead—and nothing else of interest or value. And no apparent interior access to the roof.

After examining the outside of the building Lee found one and only one service access ladder. He climbed the ladder slowly. The ladder had seen better days, so Lee didn't want to hit a bad rung and take a fall. Lee's right knee had also seen better days, and the leg brace he wore didn't help much, so he wouldn't be setting any speed records climbing even the best of ladders.

The roof would provide a satisfactory place to make camp for the night. This building was the tallest on the block, so it'd give him a good vantage point to observe the surrounding area. A two-foot wall ran the edge of the roof, so no one would be able to see him from the ground while he was lying down. And zombies were too dumb to climb ladders, so he didn't have to worry about any trouble from ghouls in the middle of the night.

It was possible someone smarter than a zombie might make his or her way up the ladder at some point, so Lee booby-trapped the ladder's top three rungs, wrapping them in short lengths of barbed wire he found in his rucksack. Lee had many skills, but his greatest might have been rucksack packing. He could squeeze a seemingly impossible amount of gear into his kit bag, and he always seemed to have the right tool for the situation.

The barbed wire on the ladder rungs was nearly invisible in the darkness. Just in case someone managed to make it past that with all his or her fingers still intact, Lee set up a simple trip wire alarm right past the ladder with some fishing line and a couple of small glass bottles.

Satisfied with the security situation, Lee made his way to the other side of roof, took off his rucksack, and settled in for the evening. He drank some water from his canteen and ate a piece of beef jerky. While he ate, he took a look around with his binoculars.

On the sidewalk across the street, Lee saw one of the ubiquitous THREAT LEVEL BLACK flyers printed by the Department of Homeland Security. Telephones and the Internet might have been a fading memory at this point, but there was still a Xerox machine or two working overtime in some government building somewhere. Lee didn't pay much attention to the flyers as they all said the same things about staying strong and holding out hope and all that. But Lee had never seen any evidence outside of the flyers that any government still existed anywhere in the United States, so he wasn't counting on a G-man or a marine to get him out of any jam he might find himself in.

Lee set his binoculars down long enough to get another piece of jerky from his bag. When he turned his attention back to the other side of the street, he noticed one of the buildings—a former thrift store by the looks of it—was occupied by a small group of zombies. Looking through the building's plate glass windows, Lee counted eight ghouls, though it was possible there were more farther back from the windows. The zombies looked to be trapped in the building. A few of them were feebly pushing on the front door, but a padlock on the door kept it firmly closed.

Another zombie was approaching from the north, making its way down the sidewalk. Lee refocused his binoculars on this new zombie and noticed the Diet Mountain Dew bottle hanging from its neck by a length of rope. It was hard to say for sure given the limited light at this hour, but Lee was pretty sure someone had deliberately arranged the rope and bottle combo and hung it on the zombie. Lee didn't bother to guess why someone would do such a thing.

The zombie was oblivious to Lee's presence, but it stopped when it reached the building with the other zombies trapped inside. The zombie pressed its rotting hands against the door and began to push, like it was trying to get inside to socialize with its zombie friends. The zombies inside increased their efforts to get out the door.

The padlock didn't budge and the door didn't open.

Lee watched the zombies across the street for a few more minutes while he finished his jerky. The whole scene was a little sad—these things had lost their humanity and their intelligence, and now they were trapped in a hopeless struggle with a locked door.

Lee returned the binoculars to his rucksack. He checked the time on his Seiko 5 wristwatch. Three minutes till midnight. He lay down and did his best to get comfortable, which was never easy these days on account of his bad knee. On top of that, this particular roof was one of the less accommodating resting spots Lee had encountered lately. He made sure his Colt M1911 pistol and his Ka-Bar seven-inch combat knife were both in their respective holsters and that his Armalite AR-15 rifle—with Bushnell thirty-two-millimeter tactical scope and a thirty-round magazine loaded with Remington .223 ammo—was within reach.

Satisfied that his base for the night was secure, Lee closed his eyes and waited for sleep to come.

Chapter 3

Meet the Eaters

The morning sunlight crept into the trunk of the silver 1998 Toyota Tercel through four small rust holes situated above the STARS FELL ON ALABAMA license plate. The Girl was in the trunk, eyes closed but not asleep. She opened an eye and saw that it was finally morning. She felt around the trunk until she found the lever to release the seatback. She folded down the seatback, exited the trunk, and made her way to the front passenger seat of the car.

The Girl reached under the seat and found her backpack. She dug through the pack, found her sunglasses, and put them on. The morning light was more bearable now. She continued to search the bag until she found a small stainless steel water bottle and a chocolate Twinkie.

The chocolate Twinkie was at least ten years old at this point, but it was still in its original airtight plastic wrapper. The Girl fiddled with the wrapper until she managed to tear it open. She took a sniff of the Twinkie. Smelled fine. Then she took a bite. It was good. Really good, in fact. The Girl knew that one day the world's remaining supply of Twinkie snack cakes—even the ones still in their original airtight plastic wrappers—would go bad and be no longer edible. But today was not that day.

While she ate, the Girl surveyed the area around the Tercel. It had once been a gravel-covered parking lot, but the gravel was overtaken by grass, weeds, and trees years ago. There were a handful of other vehicles in the lot: a 1987 Chrysler LeBaron, a lifted 4x4 pickup truck, another pickup truck that had been turned into a convertible via some questionable after-market body work, and a wrecked single-engine airplane, tail number N99NH. The airplane was missing its propeller and both its front wings, but it still had an occupant in its cockpit: the remains of the pilot, a macabre skeleton clothed in a tattered, sun-bleached leather aviator jacket.

The Girl reached into the right front pocket of her faded blue jeans and retrieved a handful of car keys. She looked through keys until she found the one for the Tercel and used it to open the glove box. From the glove box she removed five bullets. Each of the bullets was a different caliber. She put the bullets in her jeans pocket, along with all of her car keys. The Girl finished her Twinkie, had another sip of water, and exited the Tercel. She checked that the passenger door was locked and started walking.

She walked past houses long abandoned. Vines covered the houses' brick and vinyl siding. The yards hadn't seen a lawnmower in a decade. November's fallen leaves covered the yards and the road. She walked past a strip mall, slowed down for a moment to look through the window of the Blockbuster video store. There were still several VHS tapes and DVDs on the shelves, more than she would have expected. Then again, electricity was hard to come by these days. For someone with a few minutes of leisure time, books were a better option.

She walked past the Publix grocery store. She knew

it'd been picked clean long ago. She walked up the hill to the movie theater. The posters outside were faded but still barely readable. She looked at the poster for *The Incredibles*. That was the last movie the Girl had seen in a movie theater. Her younger sister had loved Pixar movies, so the Girl's father had taken her and her sister to see *The Incredibles* opening weekend. The Girl, thirteen years old at the time, liked to protest that she was too grown up for kids' movies, but now she would happily admit that *The Incredibles* was terrific. She missed going to the movies, getting popcorn and candy and oversized cups of Coca-Cola. She missed her sister. She missed her father.

Posters for three horror movies hung outside the theater: *The Grudge*, *Seed of Chucky*, and *Saw*. The Girl hadn't seen any of these movies, but the thought of facing a Japanese ghost or a homicidal toy didn't seem that scary to her. The *Saw* movie, which she had heard was about someone capturing people and torturing them . . . that scared her, because that sort of thing was all too common now.

A fallen traffic light lay at the intersection of Kentucky Avenue and Highway 31. As she walked past it, the Girl noticed how much bigger it looked up close. She made her way past another strip mall and crossed a hill into another abandoned residential area. One building stood apart from the others, a neat gray concrete and steel fortress among the overgrown ranch houses, split-levels, and bungalows. The Girl walked up to this building and knocked three times on the imposing steel door. Each knock rang out with a loud clang.

To the right of the door was a small opening covered in steel mesh. Through the opening, the Girl could hear the sound of approaching footsteps. Then a man addressed her.

"Welcome to Trader Bob's!" the man said. "In the interest of customer privacy and safety, we don't use real names here at Trader Bob's. Customers are assigned a number." This was more than fine as far as the Girl was concerned. She could count on one hand the number of people she'd shared her real name with in the past ten years.

"And my name isn't actually Bob," the man said. "Also, in case you haven't noticed, these are post-apocalyptic times, so your money is no good here. Your money is probably no good anywhere. Except maybe as kindling for a fire. Anyway, at Trader Bob's we traffic only in goods, services, and information."

The Girl waited a few moments to make sure the man was through with his disclaimers before replying.

"Morning, Bob. It's Seventy-Seven." This was not the Girl's first visit to Trader Bob's.

"Seventy-Seven! How you living, girl?"

Bob enjoyed making small talk. Considering how rare non-lethal human interaction was these days, that was understandable. The Girl played along.

"Hand to mouth, Bob. Hand to—"

"Hey," Bob said, interrupting the Girl. "Duck down for me for a second."

The Girl complied. As she did, she turned to look over her shoulder. A hundred feet away, a zombie had wandered out from behind a house and was shambling down the street toward Bob's establishment. The ghoul must have been downwind from the Girl. Otherwise, she would have smelled it already.

Metal slid against metal as a small slot in the door at about eye level opened. The Girl looked up to see the barrel of a sniper rifle peek out through the slot. The Girl winced as she plugged her ears with her fingers.

BLAM. The rifle fired. A fraction of a second later, the approaching zombie's head exploded in a fountain of blood, brains, and bone. The zombie's already wobbly knees buckled, and the creature fell to the street with a thud.

The rifle went back inside. "Sorry about that," Bob said. "So what can I do you for?" The Girl looked around to make sure the coast was indeed clear. Then she stood back up and retrieved the bullets from her pocket. She showed the bullets to Bob through the still-open slot in the door.

"All right, all right. Cool. So what do you want for these?" Bob asked.

"A fourteen-millimeter spark plug," the Girl said.

* * *

The Girl had been working on the dirt bike for a few weeks now. She'd found a book on small engine repair, and between scavenging and trading she thought she had the motorcycle almost ready to go.

The two-wheeler still wasn't much to look at, but that was for the best. If the bike appeared valuable in the least, someone bigger, stronger, or better-armed would take it, and there wouldn't be a damn thing the Girl could do about it.

Replacing the spark plug was, in theory, the bike repair project's final task. But first the Girl had to remove the old spark plug. She was trying to loosen the old plug with a crescent wrench but wasn't having much luck.

Somewhere outside the former Express Oil Service Center that currently served as the Girl's garage, something made a noise. The Girl stopped trying to loosen the spark plug. She held her breath while she strained to hear. Footsteps. Coming her way. She exited the garage, walked around the corner, and took a cautious peek behind the building.

Across the street, a blonde woman was cowering behind a rusted-out BMW station wagon. She was being stalked by a lean, muscular man. Based on the tattoos on the man's face, the Girl assumed his intentions were not good. The Girl tightened her grip on her wrench.

The tattooed man knelt, looked under the BMW, realized his prey was on the other side. He smiled as he quietly walked around the front of the car. Not quietly enough. The blonde woman realized she'd been found. The man reached the other side of the car and looked down at the woman. The blonde woman slowly stood, took a cautious step backwards. The man matched her move with a single step forward.

The Girl readied herself. When the tattooed man's inevitable attack came, she'd do her best to defend the blonde woman. He had a twelve inches on the Girl and a hundred pounds, but the Girl had a wrench and the element of surprise. Hopefully the blonde woman would be of some use in the fray as well.

Then the blonde woman unzipped her jacket and exposed her bare breasts to the tattooed man.

The Girl loosened her grip on the wrench as the blonde woman and tattooed man embraced in a deep kiss. The Girl rolled her eyes and quietly made her way back to the garage entrance. She arrived there to find three men and one petite but fierce-looking woman standing around her motorcycle.

The cleanest-cut of the four sized the Girl up, then greeted her. "How's it going?"

The Girl gritted her teeth. She knew she should immediately turn around and run away. But she'd spent so much time on the bike. She wasn't willing to abandon it just yet. Her reply was noncommittal. "It's going."

The clean-cut man pointed at the wrench in the Girl's right hand. "So. You a mechanic?"

"No. Unfortunately."

"Clint here knows a thing or two about mechanic stuff. Ain't that right, Clint?"

The man with the handlebar mustache knelt down and took a closer look at the motorcycle. He looked back at the Girl and grinned, showing a mouthful of rotten teeth. "Yeah, Jim," he said to the clean-cut man. "A thing or two."

"You ask him nice," Jim said, "he'd probably give you his professional opinion."

"Probably," Clint said.

The Girl had decided to cut her losses. She replied, "No thanks." She was just about to turn and run when Jim pointed past her. He said, "Alice and Barry, though, they don't know shit about much of anything except maybe playing grabass."

The Girl turned to see the Barry and Alice—the tattooed man and blonde woman the Girl had observed moments earlier—standing a few feet behind her. Barry had a hand on his knife, a much larger knife than the one the Girl carried on her belt. Worse, Alice had a samurai sword strapped to her back. It didn't look any better in the other direction. Jim had a revolver and a billy club, Clint had revolver, the petite woman had a small rifle, and the other guy carried a bloodstained Louisville Slugger baseball bat. The Girl was woefully outnumbered and outgunned.

"So tell me," Jim said. "You get this thing running, you gonna start up a motocross league or—"

The Girl didn't let him finish. If these clowns were going to kill her, she'd just as soon they get it over with. "Leaving," she said.

Jim raised an eyebrow. "Leaving town?"

"Leaving town. Leaving the state. Heck, I might leave the country, see what's going on in Mexico these days."

"Wait a minute. Are you telling me that you don't want to spend the rest of your life—as short as that life might be, considering the post-zombie-apocalypse state of things—right here? Who wouldn't want to live here? It's a beautiful place."

"Alabama the Beautiful," Clint said. "What they used to call it."

"Used to?" Jim asked. "Shit. That's what I still call it." Jim smiled and stood up extra straight, like he was starring in a television commercial for the state tourism board. "Alabama the Beautiful."

In a single quick move, the Girl turned to face Barry

while swinging her wrench. The wrench connected with Barry's nose. He let out a yelp of pain and started to fall. Blood was pouring from his nose.

Before Barry hit the ground, the Girl lowered her head, took three steps, and tackled Alice like a pro football player. The tackle took the wind out of Alice. She hit the ground hard. The Girl rolled off of Alice and was back on her feet a half-second later. Alice tried to take a breath but only managed a gasp. The girl disappeared around the corner of the garage.

Jim sighed. He addressed Clint and the petite woman and the other guy. "Let's go get her."

As the Girl ran, she did her best to assess the situation. She had a head start, maybe five seconds. How long would it last? How fast were her pursuers? Barry and Alice at this point, probably not so fast. But the others . . . she couldn't guess. What if they had a motor vehicle of some sort? That wouldn't be good. And what if the Girl, in her panic, ran into somebody worse than the group chasing her. In the Girl's experience, no matter how bad a situation might be, it could always get worse.

The Girl took a left at an intersection and continued running down the sidewalk until she saw the zombie. She stopped right before she ran into it. The zombie ignored the Girl. It was only interested in opening the door to the building next to the sidewalk.

The Girl looked through the building's plate glass windows to see what had so thoroughly captured the zombie's attention. More zombies were inside. Maybe a dozen. The Girl's lead had dropped a second at this point. She decided to risk another two or three seconds. She shoved the zombie at the door out of the way. At the time, she didn't notice the twenty-ounce Diet Mountain Dew bottle hanging from the zombie's neck by a length of rope. Then she went to work on the padlock with her wrench. She hit the lock once. Twice. She heard footsteps in the distance, getting closer.

That would be Jim and company. The zombie she'd just shoved regained his footing and was now more interested in the Girl.

The third time the Girl hit the padlock with her wrench it broke open. The Girl went back to running as the door opened and the zombies began to exit the building.

Clint rounded the corner, followed by Jim and the others, with Alice and Barry bringing up the rear. Alice was still struggling to catch her breath, and Barry's nose was still bleeding. Clint saw the zombies exiting the building and stopped. He scanned the area and didn't see the Girl. Clint looked back at Jim and the others, smiled his rotten smile. Then Clint turned his attention back to the zombies. He reached into his pocket and retrieved a set of brass knuckles. He slid the knuckles onto his right hand, then ran toward the group of zombies. Jim and the others followed.

A second later, Clint hit one of the zombies in the side of the head with the brass knuckles. The zombie fell to the ground, dazed from the shot to its head. Clint knelt, one knee on the zombie's chest in case it tried to move. Then Clint delivered a savage series of blows to the zombie's head with the brass knuckles until the zombie's skull cracked open.

Jim joined the brawl two steps behind Clint. Jim knocked a couple of the ghouls to the ground with his billy club. Alice hadn't totally recovered from her encounter with the Girl, but she was still able to swing her sword. She decapitated two zombies in short order.

Barry stabbed one of the zombies in the eye with his knife. The petite woman attacked a zombie with her rifle. She didn't shoot the zombie—she held the rifle by the barrel and swung it like a bat.

Across the street and three stories up, Lee watched through his binoculars as more zombies exited the building and Jim and Clint and friends beat, slashed, and stabbed those zombies into submission. Lee turned his attention farther down the sidewalk. The zombie with the plastic bottle hanging from its neck had wandered away from the melee and was slowly making its way down the sidewalk.

Lee heard a scream. He turned his attention back to the fight as Jim pulled a zombie off the petite woman, clubbed it in the head. The petite woman's neck was bleeding. The zombie had bitten her.

The petite woman looked at Jim pleadingly. Jim frowned. The bite wound was deep. Nasty. The woman was infected for sure. In a day or two, three at the outside, she'd be another mindless zombie.

Jim apologized for what he was about to do. "Sorry, babe," he said. Then he beat the petite woman to death with his billy club.

At the end of the block, just around the corner and out of sight from Jim and company, the Girl waited. She knew the zombies would distract her pursuers. She hoped they might also eliminate those pursuers. But, other than the petite woman, her pursuers were all still standing, and all but one of the zombies had been felled.

That last zombie had made its way to the end of the block and turned the corner to see the Girl. The Girl took a step back. She was about to run when she noticed the Diet Mountain Dew bottle hanging from the zombie's neck. She looked closer . . . there was a rolled-up piece of paper inside the bottle.

A gunshot rang out. A bullet hit the zombie's head. Blood and brain flew everywhere. The Girl shielded her face. The zombie fell to the ground. The Girl thought about running again, but she couldn't. She wanted that soda bottle.

The Girl cautiously peeked around the corner. She looked at Jim. He was holstering his revolver. Barry noticed the Girl. He watched as she removed her knife from its sheath. Barry held up his own knife. "You wanna tussle, girl?" he asked. "Come on over here, and we'll tussle."

The Girl ignored Barry's taunt. Her attention was on the rope around the felled zombie's neck. She knelt, quickly cut through the rope, and took the plastic Diet Mountain Dew bottle.

"You gonna shoot her, you better do it now," Clint said to Jim.

Jim put a hand on his revolver, considered it for a moment. "Nah," he said. "I want her alive."

The Girl ran, disappearing back around the corner.

On the roof of the building across the street, Lee saw that the Girl was safe—for the moment at least—and set down his rifle.

Barry knelt next to one of the felled zombies. He scalped the zombie, removing the rotting skin and dirty hair from the top of the zombie's skull. Then Barry used the butt of his knife handle to crack the skull open like a melon. He dug into the skull with his knife and scooped out a handful of the zombie's brains. Barry presented the brains to Clint.

Clint pointed at Jim. "The boss eats first," Clint said.

"Damn straight," Jim said.

Jim took the zombie brains from Barry and crammed them into his mouth. He chewed them up quickly and swallowed with a gulp.

Lee watched through his binoculars as Barry served up fresh brains to Clint and the others. Folks didn't call these guys Zombie Eaters for nothing.

* * *

The Girl ran. A mile. Another mile. She slowed down long enough to look over her shoulder. It didn't look like anyone was following her.

She ran another mile anyway.

Chapter 4

Lonely Rats

According to the manufacturer, the color of the Honda Accord was "deep velvet blue pearl." After ten years of exposure to the elements on account of it being parked in the same spot all that time, no one would accuse its finish of being particularly deep or velvety. Or blue for that matter.

The Girl didn't care about the color. It was one of several cars parked in various lots and fields in central Alabama that she called home. The Accord didn't have the most spacious trunk of the cars in her collection, but it was roomier than the Tercel she'd spent the previous night in.

Derelict sedans were all over the place. Outside of the rare Maserati or Bentley, the cars were generally ignored. This made them good places for hiding. Considering how hard gasoline was to come by, they weren't much good for driving. That's why the Girl had been restoring the motorcycle—she figured it would deliver significantly better gas mileage than any car she could find.

The trunk of a car wasn't impregnable. But it would keep out zombies and wild animals, and any human trying to break into a car would make enough noise that the Girl would at least have fair warning.

A couple of years earlier, the Girl was in a relationship with a member of the Detroit Defenders militia. The Defenders had taken over the upper levels of a ten-story condominium building. No electricity meant no working elevators, so the only route to attack the Defenders was the building's single stairwell. A simple locked door kept the zombies out, and any agressors smart enough to get past the door were scared away with a couple of molotov cocktails thrown down the stairs.

The Detroit Defenders never did much defending. They spent most of their time getting stoned and listening to Kiss records. As much as the Girl enjoyed sleeping in an actual bed at night in an actual condo, there was a limit to how many times a day she could listen to "Rock and Roll All Nite." So on one morning that followed a particularly late night of partying by her boyfriend and the other Defenders, the Girl woke up early, left the condo for the last time, and started looking for cars she could call home.

The trunk of the Accord was dimly lit thanks to the Girl's small flashlight. She was trying to get the rolled-up piece of paper out of the plastic bottle. It was proving more difficult than expected. Finally, the Girl cut the bottom out of the bottle with her knife. She unrolled the piece of paper and shone her flashlight on it. It was one of the Department of Homeland Security flyers. The Girl read the familiar text.

THREAT LEVEL BLACK

THE DEPARTMENT OF HOMELAND SECURITY
IS WORKING UNDER THE COMMAND OF
PRESIDENT GEORGE W. BUSH TO RESOLVE
THE REANIMATED CORPSE ("ZOMBIE")
CRISIS AND REESTABLISH THE FEDERAL

GOVERNMENT. THE UNITED STATES WILL
SOON RETURN TO ITS RIGHTFUL PLACE AS
THE GREATEST NATION ON EARTH.

IN THE MEANTIME, YOUR VIGILANCE AND
LOYALTY ARE APPRECIATED. FOR MORE
INFORMATION, CALL 1-800-555-USA1.

The seal of the Department of Homeland Security with its eagle and shield was printed below the text at the bottom of the flyer.

For a moment the Girl was annoyed. She'd gone to some amount of trouble to retrieve a flyer that could be found almost anywhere. There was, in fact, one under the windshield wiper blade of her Tercel. Then the Girl turned over the flyer and found the note written on the other side.

Dear Sir or Madam,

I am a scientist. Having theorized that a virus of some sort is reanimating the dead as zombies, I began investigating the possibility of a vaccine. I traveled to the town where the first zombie sighting was reported in 2004. That town is Thorsby, Alabama, approximately fifty miles south of Birmingham.

Upon reaching Thorsby, I was abducted. I am now being held captive somewhere in the bowels of the Thorsby Powerhouse by a man who calls himself "The Chief." For reasons I do not understand, the Chief has accused me of being an agent sent to Thorsby to spy on him. As punishment, the Chief plans to execute me on November 20, 2014.

If you find this letter, please deliver it to the Vulcan Alliance. Hopefully my associates there can mount a rescue campaign in time to sa—

That's all the Girl could read. The bottle that carried the note had not been capped, and the rest of the note was smeared and illegible from water damage.

She hadn't seen a calendar in years, but the Girl did her best to keep up with the date, at least the month and the year. Most of the traditions of civilized society were difficult or impossible to carry on these days, but you didn't need a Cray supercomputer for basic time-keeping. The Girl knew it was November 2014, and she was pretty sure it was the nineteenth day of the month.

There wasn't much time. Worst case, the execution would happen at midnight on the twentieth. The Girl figured she had three or four hours to find the Vulcan Alliance folks. That would give them ten or so hours to make and execute a rescue plan.

What if this scientist was already dead? That was actually the worst case. It also occurred to the Girl that this note could be some kind of prank. But that seemed unlikely. No one had time for much pranking these days.

If there was a chance, even a slight one, that she might contribute to the rescue of a scientist working on an anti-zombie vaccine . . . the Girl had to take that chance.

* * *

Trader Bob didn't have any information about the Vulcan Alliance, at least none he considered worth the chocolate Twinkie that the Girl offered in payment. He had heard some reports that the Alliance operated out of Birmingham and relayed that info to the Girl pro bono.

The city of Birmingham covered 150 square miles, give or take. The area considered "downtown" Birmingham was smaller, twenty or thirty square miles, but that was still a lot of ground for one person to cover. The odds that the Girl would find the Vulcan Alliance's base of operations in time were not good.

She walked north toward Birmingham anyway.

After her encounter with the Zombie Eaters earlier, the Girl did her best to keep a low profile on her journey. She followed Highway 31, but she avoided the actual road, sticking to the woods that had begun to encroach on the highway over the course of the past decade.

The Girl walked past the hospital and the shopping mall. After the woods thinned when she crossed Shades Creek Parkway, she continued north via side streets and alleys.

When the Girl reached Red Mountain—which wasn't much of a mountain, it was really more of a ridge—and began walking uphill, she returned to the woods. On the other side of the ridge, she exited the woods and stepped out onto Arlington Avenue. There were a few one and two-story buildings in the area. Most of the buildings' windows were broken, and the surrounding woods were slowly overtaking the buildings.

The Girl could barely make out a sign on one of the buildings:

BIRMINGHAM WELC ME CENTER

The Girl approached the building, took a closer look at the sign. She found the missing *o* from *welcome* on the ground.

All that remained of the glass door at the entrance of the Welcome Center was an aluminum frame, wrapped in vines. The Girl approached the entrance and looked inside. The door led to a lobby area that was in surprisingly good shape—there was a thick layer of dust on everything, but the ceiling and floor were still intact.

The Girl entered the lobby and approached the desk at the center of the room. The desk was covered with old brochures of local places of interest: the Civil Rights museum, Sloss Furnaces, the Sixteenth Street

Baptist Church . . . the Girl picked up a brochure for Vulcan Park and Museum.

VULCAN IS THE LARGEST CAST-IRON STATUE
IN THE WORLD AND IS THE SYMBOL OF
BIRMINGHAM, ALABAMA, REFLECTING
THE CITY'S ROOTS IN THE IRON AND STEEL
INDUSTRY. THE FIFTY-SIX-FOOT TALL STATUE
DEPICTS THE ROMAN DEITY VULCAN, GOD
OF THE FIRE AND FORGE. VISIT THE VULCAN
PARK AND MUSEUM TODAY!

The Girl studied the brochure's photo of the bearded god, his spear pointed skyward. She wondered if it was that simple, if the Vulcan Alliance was working out of the old Vulcan Park?

Bang.

The Girl instinctively ducked and moved away from the door when the shot rang out. After she had a moment to think about it, she wasn't sure the sound came from outside.

Bang. Bang.

The sound was coming from beneath her. And maybe it wasn't a gun.

Thud-thud-bang. Thud-thud-bang. There was a rhythm to the sounds. Like a drumbeat.

Then an electric guitar started up and the Girl realized the *thud-thud-bang* actually was a drumbeat.

The drums and guitar went silent again. The Girl took a cautious peek outside to make sure no one had taken an interest in the noise. She took another look at the Vulcan brochure, put it in her bag, and turned her attention back to the lobby.

The Girl walked past the brochure table to the wooden door on the opposite side of the lobby. She pushed the door open and saw it led to a stairwell. Then a red incandescent bulb next to the stairwell door lit up. The Girl almost giggled. It was silly to think that the red light was some kind of sign, telling her where to go. But it sure seemed that way.

The electric guitar started up again. An electric bass joined in, followed eight beats later by the drums. The Girl walked down the stairs. The music grew louder with each step.

At the bottom of the stairs, the Girl opened another door and walked into a basement room with cinder-block walls and a concrete floor. A three-piece rock band was set up on a low wooden stage on the other side of the room. The young women playing guitar and bass were watching each other and didn't notice the Girl slowly walking toward the stage. The guy playing drums did notice the Girl. He stopped playing, pulled a pistol from his back jeans pocket, stood up, and aimed at the Girl.

The woman playing guitar stopped playing, yelled at the drummer. "What the shit, Chet?"

Then the bass player saw the Girl. She picked up the pistol that was sitting on the music stand in front of her and took aim at the Girl. "Uh, Janie," she said, motioning to the Girl with her pistol. The guitarist turned to see the Girl. She drew a pistol from her back pocket. Now there were three guns aimed at the Girl. The Girl raised her hands to show she wasn't armed.

"Aw, damn it!" Janie said to the Girl. "That was a good take."

The Girl was confused. "What?"

"Didn't you see the red light?"

The Girl nodded.

"The red light means tape is rolling."

The Girl grinned sheepishly and shrugged.

"Everybody knows that! Doesn't everybody know that, Sarah?"

The bass player nodded.

Chet put his pistol back in his pocket and stepped away from his drum kit. The Girl slowly lowered her hands after Janie and Sarah put their guns away.

"Did you say tape?" the Girl asked.

"Yeah, tape," Sarah said. "We're recording an album."

"A double album, actually," Janie said.

Headphones, a mixing board, and a reel-to-reel tape machine sat on a table at the side of the stage. Chet put on the headphones and pressed a button on the tape machine. The tape made a whirring sound as it rewound, then stopped with a click. Chet hit another button on the machine. As the music played back through the headphones, he adjusted knobs and sliders on the mixing board.

The Girl had so many questions. She wasn't sure where to start. "Where are you guys getting electricity?"

Sarah pointed toward the ceiling. "Solar cells on the roof. Pretty efficient. We usually have enough juice to run the tape recorder and amps and lights for two or three hours a day."

"Doesn't the music attract zombies? Gangs?"

"Zombies aren't so bad," Janie said, "at least during the day. And they don't like rock music, so they keep their distance. The only gangs around here are the Zombie Eaters, and we pay them off to leave us alone."

"What do you pay them with?"

"Weed," Sarah said.

"You mean like marijuana? That grows everywhere these days."

"That grass is weak," Sarah said. She reached into her pocket and pulled out a Ziplock bag full of green, sticky buds. "We pay off the Eaters with the good shit. You wanna smoke a bowl, see for yourself?"

"No, thanks," the Girl said.

Chet rewound the tape, started it rolling again, fiddled some more with the knobs and sliders.

"Look," Janie said. "As much as I'd like to stand around playing twenty questions, we've got a double album to record."

"Oh, right," the Girl said. "Actually, just one more question. Why are you guys recording an album—"

Janie corrected her. "Double album."

"Why are you guys recording a double album," the Girl asked, "when everything is all . . . post-apocalyptic or whatever?"

Janie smiled. "Anybody lucky enough to have electricity or an old Victrola, it's been like forever since they got a new album."

"I guess," the Girl said.

"So we're recording now. Laying down a bunch of new tracks. Then one day, things turn around. Somebody finds a zombie cure, society starts coming back. Then record stores start coming back, then everybody's all, 'yeah, these old albums are great, but I wanna hear something new.'"

The Girl wasn't totally convinced. But she played along. "OK."

Janie's eyes lit up. "Boom. That's when we release our double album. None of the other bands have any new music ready. Zero competetion."

"It's gonna be huge," Sarah said.

"It'll probably be the biggest thing since Nirvana did *Nevermind*," Janie said.

The Girl grinned. She was pretty sure Janie and Sarah were delusional, but she had to admire their optimism. And were the women's dreams of rock and roll fame and fortune really any less realistic than the Girl's desire to help out the mysterious scientist who was trying to save the world?

Sarah took a cassette tape off her music stand and threw it to the Girl. The Girl examined the tape. Handwritten on it in black Sharpie:

"EVIDENCE"

BY LONELY RATS

B/W "HEAD WOUND"

"Couple songs for you," Sarah said. "Consider it an advance single."

Chapter 5

Vulcan's Spear

As the Girl made her way up Twenty-First Street and got her first glimpse of Vulcan Park, she let herself get a little excited. She'd come here looking for the Vulcan Alliance on a hunch, but seeing Vulcan Park ahead of her, she realized it would make a great base of operations for a militia group.

Vulcan Park was located on a part of Red Mountain that, though still not much of a mountain, was at least a decent-sized hill. And Vulcan itself—at 56 feet tall it was the largest cast-iron statue in the world—stood atop a 123-foot-tall pedestal. The observation deck on that pedestal offered an expansive view of the late, great city of Birmingham, Alabama. Someone on that pedestal armed with a sniper rifle—or even a set of binoculars—would have a significant tactical advantage over any enemies approaching on the ground.

With that in mind, the Girl kept a constant eye on the pedestal as she got closer to Vulcan Park. If she found herself in a shooter's gunsights, she was ready to throw up her hands and surrender. But by the time she reached the entrance to the park proper, where Twenty-Second Street met Valley Avenue, she still hadn't seen any sign of life on the pedestal beneath the great statue. Or anywhere else in the area for that matter. She walked up the hill, across the old visitor parking lot, and into the single-story brick building adjacent to the Vulcan statue.

If not for the sign on the door, the Girl might not have realized the building was the park gift shop. The display cases, merchandise shelves, and wall hangers had all been picked clean. A closer look around the room turned up a cash register on the floor behind the checkout counter. The register made a little dinging sound when the Girl opened the cash drawer. It was empty save a handful of coins.

The Girl also found two souvenir items in a dark corner of the room: a BIRMINGHAM: THE MAGIC CITY T-shirt that was crusty with dirt and dried blood and a 1:100 scale replica of the Vulcan statue. The Girl held up the replica to the window and looked past it to the real statue outside. The likeness was pretty good. The Girl set Tiny Vulcan down on one of the desolate merchandise shelves for the next tourists who came through looking for a souvenir of their visit to Birmingham.

There were three doors at the back of the room: one each for the men's and women's restrooms, and one marked EMPLOYEES ONLY. The Girl opened the third door, which led to a darkened hallway. The Girl fished around her bag and found her flashlight. Right after she turned it on, she was startled by a noise, a dull thud. She drew the knife from the sheath on her belt and took a defensive stance. Whatever made the sound was at the other end of the hall. She walked cautiously in that direction.

The hallway opened into the gift shop employee break room. Sunlight came into the room through a high window, so the Girl put her flashlight back into her bag. By the looks of things, someone had been using the break room as a barracks—the floor was littered with old mattresses and sleeping bags. One wall was covered with metal storage lockers. A man in a poncho and cowboy hat was looking through one of the lockers. He turned to face the Girl, showed her his rifle.

"You know," he said, "there's an old saying."

"Yeah," the Girl said. "Don't bring a knife to a gunfight." She slowly put her knife back in its sheath.

The cowboy opened the next locker and looked inside. "A bunch of guys calling themselves the Vulcan Alliance, you think they'd at least have some *Star Trek* tapes."

The Girl raised an eyebrow. "I think Vulcan is the big statue, not—"

The cowboy didn't let her finish. "Yeah, yeah, I know."

"You're looking for tapes?" the Girl asked.

"Looking for movies. And TV shows. Tapes, DVDs. I'll take a LaserDisc."

The cowboy took another look at the Girl. Then he held his hands about twelve inches apart. "Probably before your time. Like a big CD with video instead of music. Not to be confused with videodisc, which was an inferior format. Just as well because I never have found a working videodisc player."

"No. I mean, yeah, I know what it is," the Girl said. "But . . . you're not part of the Alliance?"

"Nope. Just scavenger-ing. That's what you're doing, right?"

The Girl dug through her bag, found the scientist's note, and showed it to the cowboy.

"Actually," the Girl said, "I was trying to deliver this note."

The cowboy grinned. "No way. You're out playing *The Postman*? Kevin Costner would be proud."

Irritated, the Girl moved closer to the cowboy and handed him the letter. "Look," she said. "This guy . . . I guess it's a guy . . . he's a scientist, part of the Vulcan Alliance, and he was working on a vaccine for the zombie virus or whatever it is, and he needed to do some research in the place where it all started, which is Thorsby, this little town—"

The cowboy looked up from the letter. "I know Thorsby."

"But when he got to Thorsby some guy called the Chief—"

"The Chief? What is he, some kind of Indian?"

The Girl shrugged. "No idea. But the Chief, he's holding this scientist prisoner. And he's gonna kill him on the twentieth of November."

"That's the tenth anniversary," the cowboy said.

"Of what?" the Girl asked.

"Zombie apocalypse. End of the world as we know it. Whatever you wanna call it."

"Really?"

"Yeah," the cowboy said. "I killed one of the first zombies that morning in my video store. And it went downhill from there. Except for Auburn winning the Iron Bowl. That was pretty great. November 20, that's like today. Or maybe tomorrow. 2012 was a leap year, right? I—"

"We should go rescue this guy."

"We should what?" the cowboy asked.

"This scientist," the Girl said. "We should go rescue him. I mean, his Vulcan Alliance buddies aren't gonna do it."

The cowboy indicated the gift shop break room. "So because I'm looting the place where he used to live, I'm supposed to lead a rescue mission?"

"You don't have to lead it," the Girl said.

The cowboy pointed at the scientist's letter. "Where'd you find this note?"

"It was in a bottle. On a rope. Tied to a zombie." Saying it out loud, the Girl felt a little silly.

The cowboy gave the note back to the Girl. "I'm not rescuing anybody."

"But he's working on a zombie vaccine!"

"Working on. Allegedly. Assuming this Chief character didn't get antsy and kill him already. Assuming that's a real note written by a real person."

The Girl frowned. "Fine. I'll rescue him myself."

"You're gonna take your knife, walk to Thorsby, infiltrate this whatever it is—"

"You don't think that's a good plan?" the Girl asked.

The cowboy couldn't believe she even asked him that. "No! It's a terrible plan. One that will more than likely get you killed before you get anywhere near Thorsby. But, hey, good luck with it."

The cowboy walked past the Girl and headed for the exit. She didn't turn to watch him leave. She just counted his steps as he moved farther away from her. Five . . . six . . . seven . . .

Seven . . .

Where was eight? The cowboy had stopped walking. Did he forget something? Was he going to offer a few more discouraging words before leaving for good? Or . . . was he having a change of heart?

The Girl was curious, but she still refused to turn and face the cowboy.

"OK, look," the Girl heard the cowboy say. She could tell by the tone of his voice, quieter, more compromising than before, that he'd had a change of heart.

"I'm not going to Thorsby," the cowboy said. "Because I'm not suicidal. But I will give you a ride as far as my place, scrounge up a gun and some ammo for you. That might keep you alive an extra hour or two."

* * *

The Girl and the cowboy made their way down the hill and through the woods on the south side of Vulcan Park.

"You have a horse?" the Girl asked.

"Yeah."

"Way out here in the woods?"

"Yeah. Can't just leave a horse standing around in a

bad part of town," the cowboy said. "Which is really any part of town. These days, a horse is worth its weight in, I don't know . . ."

"Ammunition?"

The cowboy considered it. "Well . . . maybe not worth that much."

The two reached the cowboy's horse. The cowboy tied his rifle to the saddle. The Girl looked at the animal in awe. She couldn't remember the last time she'd seen a horse.

"Can I pet her?" the Girl asked.

The cowboy gave the horse an affectionate pat on the head. "Him," the cowboy said. "And, yes, you can pet this handsome fella."

The Girl cautiously petted the horse's nose and mane. The cowboy got himself up in the saddle, then extended a hand to the Girl.

"I'm Chuck, by the way," he said. "What's your handle?"

The Girl grinned sheepishly. "I'd rather not say."

Chuck nodded. "Girl with no name. Cool."

The Girl still hadn't accepted Chuck's hand. She looked at him suspiciously. "You're not gonna take me back to your place and kill me or . . . it's just most everybody I meet these days wants to kill me or eat me or—"

"Two minutes ago you invited me on a road trip."

"Rescue mission," the Girl said.

"And now you're getting cautious?"

"Sorry," the Girl said. "I'm impulsive sometimes."

"If I was going to kill you, I would have just shot you in the gift shop. I don't need that kind of mess at home."

Again Chuck reached out his hand to the Girl. She finally took it and made her way up on the saddle behind Chuck.

"You're not going to stab me in the back are you?" he asked her sarcastically.

Chuck and the Girl rode out of the woods and on down the hill to the park's main exit where Twenty-

First Street met Valley Avenue. They didn't look back at Vulcan or the gift shop. If they had, they might have seen Clint. He was standing on the observation deck on the great statue's pedestal, watching Chuck and the Girl intently through a pair of binoculars.

Clint smiled his disgusting smile. "There's my little rabbit."

* * *

As afternoon gave way to dusk, Chuck and the Girl continued south on the horse.

"What's your horse's name?" the Girl asked.

"Carol," Chuck said.

"I thought you said the horse is a boy."

"He is," Chuck said. "Named after Carol Reed, the guy that directed *The Third Man*."

"I thought Orson Welles directed that movie."

"Nope. Reed. Welles is in it though. And he's great. As usual."

"So you call it the zombie apocalypse?" the Girl asked.

"Yeah. I think I got that from DJ Dan. You know Dan? 'King of the Pirate Airwaves'?"

"I don't know him personally. But I've heard him on the radio. Instead of the zombie apocalypse, why not zombie armageddon?"

"Armageddon implies an epic battle between good and evil," Chuck said.

"Humans versus zombies."

"Zombies aren't evil," Chuck said. "They're just dumb. Calling this situation armageddon is almost as bad as calling a movie about people fighting a giant space rock *Armageddon*. Which happened."

"Better than *Deep Impact*," the Girl said. "I mean, the porn parody of *Deep Impact* would be called *Deep Impact*."

The Girl had a point. "Yeah," Chuck said. "But it's

fairly accurate. You know, there's a Sam Neill movie that's sort of about armageddon."

"Is it called *Armageddon*?" the Girl asked.

"No. It's called *Omen III: The Final Conflict.*"

"Which is an awesome name for a movie," the Girl said.

Chuck agreed. "Totally."

Chapter 6

Home Invasion

During the spring and fall, tornadoes were common in Alabama, especially in the state's more rural areas. People in those areas would often build an underground storm cellar for protection during stormy weather, especially if their house didn't have a basement.

After tying up his horse and cranking a small generator, Chuck led the Girl down the stairs into the storm cellar which Chuck had called home for the last few months. The Girl surveyed the small room. There were two 32-inch Sony Trinitron televisions set up side-by-side against one wall, along with an assortment of VHS VCRs, several DVD players, a Betamax machine, and a Pioneer LaserDisc player. Tapes and discs were stacked floor-to-ceiling against the other three walls. Furnishings were sparse: a futon, a couple of metal folding chairs of the high school cafeteria variety, a table covered with videotapes and DVDs, and a few bookshelves loaded down with still more tapes and discs.

"Wow," the Girl said. "You are really into movies." She sat down on the futon, bathed in the blueish glow of static from the two TVs. "Guess that explains your Maynard T. Krebs-meets-Clint Eastwood look."

Chuck straightened his cowboy hat and stroked his goatee. "So you know Nick at Nite and spaghetti westerns. Be careful or I might fall in love with you."

The Girl rolled her eyes. "Be still my heart."

Chuck pressed the record button on one of the VCRs and the play button on another. The picture on both TVs changed over from static to the opening of *The Phantom Planet*, a black and white sci-fi movie from 1961.

Chuck looked through a plastic storage bin near the TV sets and retrieved a small .22 caliber revolver and a handful of bullets. He handed the Girl the gun and ammo and sat down on a metal folding chair next to the futon. The Girl loaded the gun making sure the first chamber was empty, then put the gun and the rest of the bullets in her bag.

The Girl noticed a bucket sitting on the concrete floor in front of the futon. It contained a few brown glass bottles. "Beer?" she asked.

"Home brew," Chuck said. "Not great, but drinkable."

"So you watch TV with a generator, but you don't have a fridge?"

"I can drink warm beer," Chuck said. "Gotta save the electricity for copying movies."

The Girl had the scientist's note in her hand. She was folding it and unfolding it absentmindedly. "You're copying the movies?"

"Somebody's got to," Chuck said. "Protect the art form for future generations and all. I mean, if there are any future generations."

The Girl glanced over at a nearby stack of movies, called out the first title that caught her eye. "*Starship Troopers* is art?"

"As a matter of fact," Chuck said, "it's a cutting satire of America's imperialist foreign policy. And, bonus,

Dina Meyer does a couple of topless scenes."

"Yeah. Well . . . seems like if your mission is to preserve the culture there are more important things you could be collecting."

"I'm supposed to save everything myself? I guarantee you right now there's some other cat holed up in a library making sure the books are safe. And there's someone else in a museum somewhere protecting paintings and statues and shit. This," Chuck said, indicating his room full of tapes and discs, "is my part."

Chuck's passionate argument for the value of cinema, even cinema of the shirtless-girls-versus-giant-bugs-from-outer-space variety, had halfway convinced the Girl that he wasn't completely full of shit.

Chuck took one of the homebrew beers from the bucket and offered it to the Girl. "Speaking of missions, you want a beer before you head out on yours?"

The Girl accepted the beer and took a swig. Yikes. Chuck's description of the beer as "drinkable" seemed charitable. She still had the note in her left hand. She showed it to Chuck, then dropped it on the futon beside him.

"You're really not interested in helping me find this guy?" the Girl asked.

"I don't know why anybody would be interested in—"

The Girl didn't let him finish. "Because it is something we can do!" she said. Her interruption came out louder than intended. "Something to try to fix things or at least stop things from getting any worse. I mean, you can't just sit here and watch movies and . . ."

"And what?" Chuck asked.

"And . . . wait it out."

"As a matter of fact," Chuck said, "I plan on doing just that."

The Girl sighed. She was so frustrated that she'd forgotten how bad the beer was. Then she took another gulp and was quickly reminded.

Chuck got up from the futon and walked over to one

of the stacks of tapes. After searching for a moment, he found the movie he was looking for and carefully dislodged it from the pile.

Chuck threw the VHS tape to the Girl. She managed to catch it with her free hand. She turned the tape over so she could read the handwritten label:

28 DAYS LATER
DANNY BOYLE
2002
113 MINUTES
UK

The Girl asked, "This is a zombie movie, right?"

"Technically not a zombie movie," Chuck said, "but it does make a relatable point. The infected in the movie are just these . . . rage monsters. Don't eat. Don't take care of themselves. Eventually, it's reasoned, they'll starve and die.

"Similarly, zombies are dead. No circulation, no blood flow. They eat, but they aren't getting nutrition or anything from it. They're walking meat. And eventually meat will rot away. So yes. I can wait it out."

The Girl considered Chuck's reasoning. She tossed the tape back to him. "OK," the Girl said. "Let me get this straight. Your plan for surviving the zombie apocalypse is based on a movie . . . that's not even really about zombies?"

"Well," Chuck said. "If you say it like that."

Before Chuck could formulate a counterargument, the room went completely dark as the televisions, lamps, and VCRs all shut down in unison. The hum of the generator outside trailed off to silence. The Girl started to say something, but Chuck shushed her.

Something was going on outside. Footsteps. The low murmur of voices. Something rattled. Then there was a loud knock at the door at the top of the stairs.

"Shit," Chuck said. He drew his pistol from its holster. He fumbled around with it in the darkness, managed to get the cylinder opened, and confirmed that each chamber contained a bullet.

More knocks at the door. Heavy knocks. Somebody was trying to force the door open. Chuck figured it wouldn't take too long. For a storm shelter, the lock on the door was pretty damn flimsy.

"You got some kind of emergency exit out of here?" the Girl asked.

"Yeah, it's just like the Batcave." Chuck said. "There's a tunnel that leads out to a fake 'road closed' barricade. From there, it's only fourteen miles to Gotham City."

Oh. He was being sarcastic. "So you don't—"

"No," Chuck said. "Because I never needed an emergency exit, because nobody ever found this place till I brought you here."

At the top of the stairs, a gunshot rang out, and the door lock finally broke. The door swung open, and moonlight flooded the bunker. Chuck quickly turned over the futon and crouched down behind it. The Girl knelt beside him.

"OK," Chuck whispered. "You hide under the stairs. I'll try to distract them, draw their fire. You see a chance to get up the stairs, take it."

The Girl just stared blankly at Chuck. His willingness to sacrifice himself to help her escape surprised her.

"Hey," Chuck whispered. "What are you waiting for? Go."

The Girl snapped out of it. She started to stand up, but Chuck grabbed her by the wrist. "Wait. Give me that beer."

The Girl gave the beer to Chuck. He took a long sip while the Girl ran over to the staircase. She had just enough time to get settled underneath the staircase when the first of the intruders came down the stairs.

Blam. The muzzle flash from Chuck's revolver lit up

the room for a fraction of a second. Chuck's bullet hit the first intruder in the knee. The intruder screamed in pain as his knee exploded in a shower of blood and bone, then he fell face first to the bottom of the stairs.

The second intruder down the stairs almost tripped over the first. "Damn it, Jake," he said. The Girl couldn't see him from her hiding place, but she recognized the voice and the syrupy southern accent—it was Clint, the Zombie Eater. Of course it was Clint. The Girl thought she'd been careful not to be followed. Not careful enough, obviously.

Clint fired a couple of rounds at Chuck from his .44 Magnum revolver. Chuck ducked behind the futon, then came back up to return fire, forcing Clint to take cover behind a bookshelf.

More Eaters made it down the stairs. If the Girl could have seen them, she would have recognized Jim and Barry. Dodging gunfire from Chuck, Jim took cover behind the bookshelf with Clint. Barry took cover behind an overturned table, then dragged Jake off the stairs. Jake let out a yelp when he landed on the concrete floor.

The last Eater down the stairs was Larry. He jumped the bottom three steps and joined Jim and Clint behind the bookshelf. There wasn't a lot of room behind the bookcase, and Larry was a pretty big guy. He offered a slightly embarrassed apology. "Uh . . . excuse me."

"Well it's a hell of a place for a shootout," Jim said, doing his best to make some space for himself while still staying out of the line of fire.

Bullets flew. Chuck emptied his revolver and reloaded. Shots fired by the Eaters shattered the screen of one of Chuck's televisions, then the other. A bullet penetrated the futon mattress and whizzed past Chuck's ear, and he realized the futon made for pretty terrible shelter. Chuck gulped down the rest of the home-brewed beer figuring he didn't want to be totally sober if he got shot.

Sparks erupted from the front panel of the LaserDisc player when another stray Eater bullet hit it. "Son of a bitch," Chuck mumbled under his breath. The wrecked televisions would be easy to replace, but good Laser-Disc players were few and far between.

Behind the table, Barry dropped his pistol. He was pale, dripping sweat. He mumbled to Jake. "I ain't feeling too good."

Jake took a peek over the edge of the table. Before he could take a shot, Chuck fired a round that almost took his head off. He ducked back down, glanced at his leg and all the blood. He looked at Barry and said, "Well I just got shot in the damn knee, so—"

Jake stopped talking when he saw Barry's eyes. The irises had lost their color. Each eye was milky white.

"Aw, man."

Barry lunged at Jake, took him to the floor. Jake screamed when Barry bit into his left arm right below the elbow.

Chuck wasn't sure what was going on, but he knew it wasn't good for the Eaters, so he fired off a few rounds, adding to the chaos. He caught a glimpse of the Girl making her way up the stairs. Chuck hoped the intruders hadn't been smart enough to leave someone at the top of the stairs to guard their rear flank.

Larry ran out from behind the bookcase. Chuck fired a couple of rounds at the staircase, hoping that would deter Larry from looking upstairs and seeing the Girl get away. Larry dove down behind the table and wrestled Barry off of Jake. The chunk of Jake's arm had apparently not satisfied Barry's appetite. Since he was so eager to eat something, Larry put the barrel of his snub-nose .38 revolver in Barry's mouth and let him eat a bullet. Barry's brains and pieces of the back of his skull sprayed all over the floor.

"Shit man," Jake said. "He bit me." Larry looked at Jake's bloody forearm, then down at his own .38.

"It's not too late," Jake said, desperation in his eyes.

"Somebody can cut my arm off." He looked over to the bookshelf. "Jim! It's not too late!"

Clint took aim at Jake. Larry realized what was happening and crawled out of the way right before Clint fired a shot from his revolver and put a bullet between Jake's eyes. Then he turned his aim to Chuck and emptied his gun into the futon. The last of the bullets penetrated the mattress and shattered Chuck's empty beer bottle.

"What's the matter?" Chuck asked. "One of your guys go zombie on you?"

"Occupational hazard," Jim said.

Chuck checked his revolver. It was empty again. And he didn't have any more ammo in his pocket.

"How about you just give us the girl—"

Chuck didn't let Jim finish. "And what, you'll let me live?"

"No," Jim said. "But we'll kill you quick. And painless."

The gunfight was over. Chuck raised his hands as a sign of surrender. He waited a moment in hopes that the Eaters would calm the hell down, then slowly got to his feet. He looked at the Eaters, wished he'd killed more than two of them, then remembered he hadn't killed any of them, he'd just shot Jake in the knee. Shit, if he could have held out a little longer, all of these clowns might have managed to kill each other.

"Now where's the girl?" Jim asked.

"No girls here," Chuck said. "I mean, except for you sorry bitches."

Clint and Larry looked at Jim to see how he would react to Chuck's taunt. Jim's thumb made its way to the hammer of his revolver but stopped short of pulling it back.

"Let's take this asshole back to the warehouse," Jim said.

Larry grabbed Chuck by the collar of his shirt and led him up the stairs. Jim followed him. Clint grabbed himself a beer from the bucket, opened it up, and took a sip. He winced at the taste, took another sip anyway.

"Clint! You coming?" Jim yelled down from outside.

"In a minute," Clint said. He stepped behind the futon. Something on the floor among the spent ammunition and scraps of mattress caught Clint's eye. He knelt and picked up a piece of paper. He unfolded it and saw the familiar THREAT LEVEL BLACK message on one side. Then Clint turned over the paper and read the scientist's note.

Outside, Jim untied Chuck's horse and climbed up in the saddle. Chuck shot him a dirty look. "Horse-thieving son of a bitch," he muttered.

Larry took Chuck's bandana and used it to blindfold Chuck. "Really?" Chuck asked.

No answer from Larry. He just gave Chuck a good shove from behind. Chuck took the hint and started walking.

"So I'll never know the location of your secret lair?" Chuck asked.

"Something like that," Larry said.

"How far am I walking? Blindfolded?"

"It's a ways," Larry said.

Chuck stumbled a bit, then regained his balance. "I'm starting to regret I didn't take a bullet during the shootout."

Chapter 7

Alone in the Dark

Whenever people are captured and blindfolded in the movies, the clever ones count their steps and listen for subtle audio clues to determine their location. That way, when they make their escape, they have some idea where they are escaping from. Ten minutes into his blind march, Chuck concluded he wasn't that clever and concentrated on not tripping and busting his ass instead of counting and whatnot.

Sometime later—an hour or so was Chuck's best guess—Larry clumsily led Chuck up a short stairway and knocked a few times on a metal door. From the sound of things, there was a party going on inside— loud rock music was playing and people were talking excitedly somewhere on the other side of that door.

A few seconds later, a voice from the other side of the door asked, "What's the password?"

"Ha ha, asshole, you're hilarious," Larry said. The door opened. Larry led Chuck inside and pushed him down a hallway in the direction of the people and music.

The hallway opened into a larger room. It was loud with music and talking, but Chuck could still make out the faint sound of an electrical generator somewhere outside.

When the people in the room noticed Larry's prisoner, several of them shouted jeers and taunts. As Larry guided Chuck through the crowded room, he took a few rough shoves from the mob.

Somewhere near the middle of the crowd, Chuck heard the loud sound of high-heeled boots moving in his direction. A hand grabbed him by the shoulder and spun him around. A woman screamed at him, "You son of a bitch, you killed my man!"

The woman was all up in Chuck's face. He could tell from her breath and the way she slurred her words that she was drunk. He could only guess she was upset about one of the idiots who got killed in the shootout at his place earlier. "Look—" he said.

Before he could finish, the woman slapped Chuck in the face. Hard. The slap got the crowd's attention. The chatter in the room, especially near Chuck, got quieter. The woman pulled Chuck closer to her and said, "I can't wait to see you die a slow, painful death."

Chuck didn't have time to reply before the woman slapped the shit out him again. Chuck didn't try to correct the woman again. He just said, "Ouch." The woman walked off. A few people in the crowd whooped and cheered, after which they went back to their partying. Larry led Chuck through the rest of the crowd and out of the room, into another hallway.

* * *

Lee had been meticulously gathering intel on the Zombie Eaters for nearly a month now. Some in his position would have gotten bored and careless and blown their cover. Not Lee—Lee was patient.

But the time for intel was over. Lee found out there wasn't much to the Eaters. The whole lot of them were a menace, plain and simple. Lee knew tonight was a big night for the Eaters, that the vast majority of them would be here in the warehouse. And tonight Lee was going to blow them all to kingdom come.

It had taken Lee about an hour to plant ten pieces of Semtex, each about the size of a baseball, around the building. Semtex was a plastic explosive, yellowish orange in color with the consistency of the Play-Doh Lee used to play with as a kid. Even with it being a big night, Lee expected to run into a lookout or two guarding the building perimeter, but he hadn't seen anyone outside. Lee stuck to the shadows anyway—better safe than sorry.

Each piece of Semtex contained a blasting cap, and all of the blasting caps were wired together in series. Lee unspooled the wire that was connected to all the caps as he walked away from the building, across the railroad tracks, and under the Red Mountain Expressway overpass. He knelt behind one of the overpass' large concrete supports and carefully connected the wire to his detonator switch.

Concentrating on the task at hand, Lee didn't hear the person approaching from behind. But he heard the click of the hammer of a revolver right behind his head. He carefully set the detonator on the ground and raised his hands. "A'ight, man," Lee said. "You got me."

"Yeah, that's right." Judging from the voice, it was a young woman who had the drop on Lee. "I mean, except for the 'man' part," she said. "What's your name, cowboy?"

"Lee."

"As in 'Robert E.'?" the woman asked.

"I guess," Lee said. "I'm not a fan of the general. I like Lee Majors better. He played the Six Million Dollar Man on the TV."

"All right, Lee-like-Majors, not Lee-like-Robert E.," the woman said. "It's time for you to take me inside your friends' warehouse and help me rescue my friend."

"I ain't got no friends in that warehouse," Lee said.

Even with a gun pointed at the back of his head, Lee spoke quietly and calmly, with an accent familiar to anyone who had spent much time in rural Alabama.

"You're not with the Zombie Eaters?"

"Naw," Lee said. "When you got the drop on me, I was about to blow up that warehouse."

"Like with dynamite or something?" the woman asked.

"Semtex."

Lee heard the woman release the hammer on the pistol and take a couple of steps back.

"Oh," she said. "But you can't. They've got Chuck in there."

Lee lowered his hands and stood up from his kneeling position. It took him a few seconds on account of his bad knee. He turned to face the woman and recognized her. It was the Girl. He'd seen her escape from the Zombie Eaters earlier that morning.

"Am I supposed to know who Chuck is?" Lee asked.

"He's my friend," the Girl said. "Well, I guess he's more of an acquaintance. But those guys have him and—"

"How'd you find this place?" Lee asked.

"After the Zombie Eaters captured Chuck, I followed them here—"

Lee interrupted the Girl again. "How many people did you follow here?"

"Like Chuck and two Zombie Eaters."

"You think it might have been smarter to try and rescue your friend when it was just you and him against a couple of Eaters?" Lee asked.

"Maybe so. How many people are in the warehouse?"

"Couple hundred," Lee said. "Give or take."

"Oh," the Girl said.

* * *

Alone in the Dark. That was a movie from the 1980s

about . . . Chuck couldn't remember exactly. Seemed like it was either a slasher movie or a home invasion movie. Chuck wasn't sure he'd ever watched it. The movie had come to mind because its title was an apt description of Chuck's situation—blindfolded and tied to a chair. Alone in the dark.

Was there another *Alone in the Dark* movie, like from the 1960s? With Audrey Hepburn as a blind woman, and there were these criminals trying to steal something from her . . . no, that was *Wait Until Dark*.

"Hello?" Chuck called out, not for the first time. No reply. Based on the echo, whatever room he was in wasn't very big. And the party was still going on—he could hear music and talking coming from elsewhere in the building.

The party music stopped. Though Chuck couldn't make out exactly what he was saying, he recognized DJ Dan's voice. So the Eaters had their radio tuned to 94.7 FM tonight.

Another song started up on the radio, then Chuck noticed another sound, something closer. Footsteps. Women, at least two, wearing high heels. The footsteps got closer and closer until they finally stopped.

Chuck waited a moment, then asked, "Anybody there?"

One of the women approached Chuck and knocked his cowboy hat off his head. "Hey!" Chuck said. The woman ignored his protest and removed his blindfold. Chuck squinted. He was sitting directly beneath a bright lightbulb. After a few seconds, his eyes adjusted to the light and he got a look at his visitors. They were both dressed provocatively—stiletto heels, fishnet stockings, and topless.

The woman who had removed his blindfold wore her black hair in a mohawk, styled high in the punk rock tradition. She took off Chuck's poncho and tossed it to the other woman.

"So," the other woman, a blonde, said. "Heard you

killed Barry and Jake."

Apparently, it was "women accuse Chuck of murder" day.

"Sister," Chuck said, "I haven't killed anybody. At least not lately."

"So your girlfriend killed them?"

"Killed who?" Chuck asked, making no attempt to hide his irritation. "The guys who broke into my place, tried to shoot me, and destroyed my LaserDisc player?"

The other woman, the one with the mohawk, asked, "What's a LaserDisc player?"

"It's like a —" Chuck started to explain, then thought better of it. "Never mind. Look, one of those guys turned into a zombie—"

"Occupational hazard," the blonde woman said.

"You guys need a new hobby," Chuck said. "That zombie bit another guy. Jake? Anyway, then the other guys shot the zombie and the guy who got bit by the zombie. So how is any of that my fault?"

Blondie bent down and got in Chuck's face. "Because none of this would have happened if it wasn't for your slut-whore girlfriend!"

"I don't have a girlfriend," Chuck said. "And no, I am not in the market for a girlfriend, so you crazy bitches stay off my dick."

❋ ❋ ❋

Outside the warehouse, the Girl followed Lee as he quietly made his way around the building, sticking to the shadows like he did when he was planting the Semtex.

The two climbed up on the cab of a derelict pickup truck. From there, they were able to get onto the warehouse roof. Lee and the Girl made their way across the roof, then into the building via a trapdoor.

The trapdoor opened into a narrow hallway. The Girl followed Lee down the hallway. Lee removed a piece of jerky from his vest pocket and took a bite. From the sounds of things, the party downstairs was getting rowdier. The two reached the end of the hallway and began making their way down a staircase.

"You got a plan?" the Girl asked.

Lee stopped and turned around to face the Girl up the steps behind him.

"I was planning to blow the place up," he said. "I thought you had the plan for rescuing what's-his-name."

"Chuck," the Girl said. "So these Zombie Eaters must have really pissed you off. I mean, they pissed me off, but I wasn't going to blow up their whole warehouse."

"Blowing up the warehouse ain't nothing personal," Lee explained. "I'm on a job. Official Militia business."

"So you're in a militia?" the Girl asked.

"I'm in *the* Militia," Lee said. He took another bite of jerky and continued down the stairs.

Chapter 8

Fight Night

The two topless women blindfolded Chuck. Again. Then they led him back out to the big room with all the people, the room where the angry woman had slapped him earlier. People seemed to pay less attention to him this time—there wasn't as much taunting from the crowd.

The women tied Chuck's left wrist to a length of rope that led to large bolt secured to the floor. They tied his right wrist to a zombie's wrist. That was Chuck's assumption. He was blindfolded, but he could still smell. And the feel of the zombie's cold, rotting flesh against Chuck's forearm was unmistakable.

Chuck gave the zombie a strong tug. If the zombie was in bad enough shape, its arm might just fall off. Apparently this zombie wasn't that bad off. Chuck's actions only agitated the zombie, who complained with some feeble, guttural moans.

Something was happening. It was subtle, but the mood of the crowd was changing, growing more excited. Then Chuck heard a man yell over the crowd and the loud rock music, "It's fight night, y'all!"

The crowd went wild. It only took Chuck a moment

to recognize the voice—it was Jim, the asshole who had led the attack on Chuck's bunker only hours earlier.

"All right, all right," Jim continued. He was close to Chuck and the zombie now. "In this corner, three-time fight night champion . . . we found him wandering a graveyard in West Blocton. Real name unknown, but around here we call him . . . Hungry Jack!"

Somebody slapped Jack the zombie and he let out an angry growl. The crowd cheered its approval.

"Tonight's challenger. The new meat," Jim said. Someone removed Chuck's blindfold and he finally got a look at his surroundings. He was, indeed, tied wrist-to-wrist to Hungry Jack the zombie. Chuck was a tall guy, but Jack was taller. The only thing keeping Jack at bay—his left wrist was anchored to the floor via a rope, just like Chuck's.

There were a couple hundred Eaters in the room, all looking at Chuck, all chanting, "Meat! Meat! Meat!" Mohawk Girl was standing behind Chuck with his blindfold in one hand and a switchblade knife in the other. Blondie was standing by Hungry Jack. When Chuck looked at her, she did a little pirouette to show off Chuck's poncho, which she was now wearing. Jim was working the crowd, looking sharp thanks to the black tuxedo jacket he'd added to his usual white T-shirt and blue jeans.

Zombies were everywhere. Incapacitated, of course. Tied to beams, tied to the walls—the Eaters were using them for decoration, like a sane person might do with a painting or a sculpture. On the other side of the room, a legless and armless zombie was strapped to a table. The poor ghoul could only watch and moan as people in the crowd dined on pieces of its flesh and organs. Chuck turned away when one of the Eaters dug out one of the table zombie's eyes with screwdriver and bit into it like it was a plum.

After the crowd calmed back down a bit, Jim asked Chuck, "What's your name, buddy?"

"Go eat a dick," Chuck said.

The crowd didn't like that. Jim smiled. "How about we eat your brains after my boy Jack here . . . jacks your shit up?"

Jim really played up the last bit, and the crowd went crazy. "Y'all know the rules. No weapons. The fight is mano a mano. Tooth and nail. Winner lives to fight again. Loser gets eaten!"

The crowd continued to roar. No one could hear Chuck when he mumbled to himself, "I guess it was just a matter of time before shit got all Thunderdome."

Mohawk Girl grabbed Chuck by the hair on the back of his head and licked his face. "Yummy," she said. "I'll definitely be rooting for the zombie."

"Put a shirt on," Chuck said.

Jim looked back at Chuck and Jack. "You guys ready?"

"Sure," Chuck said. Hungry Jack just stared blankly ahead and moaned.

Jim turned to face the crowd and raised his hands high in the air. "Then let's get it on!"

The crowd cheered. Jim got clear of Chuck and Hungry Jack. Blondie and Mohawk Girl cut the ropes that restrained Chuck and the zombie. As soon as Hungry Jack was loose, he tried to take a bite out of Chuck's right hand, the one that was bound to Jack's right hand. Chuck managed to stun Jack with a left hook courtesy of his now free hand. Chuck had avoided a bite that would most certainly prove deadly. But he wasn't much of a brawler, and Jack was surprisingly strong for a zombie. Chuck didn't like his odds.

Chuck tried to use his free hand to untie himself from Jack. No luck—the knot was tight. Chuck put a knee in Jack's stomach, but it didn't have any effect. Of course. Nothing outside of head blows was likely to bother the zombie.

Hungry Jack tried again to take a bite out of Chuck. Chuck stumbled, almost fell, then he got an idea. He swung Jack out and away. Pivoted. Continued swinging

Jack, so the two were moving in a circle. Centrifugal force was keeping the zombie at bay.

This application of simple physics seemed to confound Hungry Jack. His growl almost sounded like a question.

The Zombie Eaters figured out Chuck's strategy and were not pleased. They started booing and hissing. Chuck grinned, taunted the crowd. "Centrifugal force, shitheads! I can do this all night!"

Someone near the front of the crowd raised a severed zombie arm and threw it at Chuck. It hit Chuck's left foot. He tripped and fell to the hardwood floor with Hungry Jack coming down on top of him. Chuck's spill excited the crowd. They cheered.

Chuck managed to get out from under Jack. He tried again to free his right hand from Jack's. Still no luck. Chuck grabbed Jack by the hair, slammed his head into the hardwood floor once. Twice. Three times. Why wouldn't this son of a bitch's skull break open?

Hungry Jack somehow turned the tables, and Chuck found himself on bottom again. Jack's face was so close to Chuck he could smell the ghoul's foul breath. The crowd cheered louder. Chuck's defeat seemed inevitable.

Then, out of nowhere, a gunshot. A bullet tore into Jim's knee and he fell to the floor. Some in the crowd noticed Jim go down, some continued cheering for Hungry Jack. Then there was another gunshot. A spectator near the front of the crowd fell to the floor when a bullet hit him in the back of the head and came out the other side, removing a large portion of his face. That got everyone's attention. Well, everyone except for Chuck, who was still trying to not get eaten.

While the crowd had been watching Chuck and Hungry Jack fight, Lee had crept into the room. He was looking down at the crowd over the scope of an AR-15 assault rifle. Lee fired a third bullet that tore into the radio. Sparks flew and the music stopped.

"A'ight!" Lee shouted. "Everybody put your hands up!"

Most of the Eaters complied and raised their hands. A few of the Eaters did not comply. Lee fired another shot that obliterated the shoulder of one of the non-compliant Eaters. That Eater fell to the floor, screaming in pain.

"Shit, that hurts!" the injured Eater said.

"I said 'everybody put your hands up!'" Lee said. "Not 'most of you put your hands up!'"

The delinquents' hands went up. Eaters whose hands were already up went up a little higher.

A machete slid across the floor, stopping next to Chuck and Jack. Chuck saw the machete, looked up to see it was the Girl who had slid it in his direction. He grabbed the machete with his free hand and planted it in Hungry Jack's skull. Jack seemed a lot less hungry after that.

From his place on the floor, Jim touched his hand to his leg where Lee had shot him. Jim winced. He held up his hand and looked at all the blood on it. Then he looked up at Lee while he addressed the other Zombie Eaters. "All right, everybody. I'm looking around, and unless my math is way off, there's just the one guy up there with a rifle and a whole bunch of us down here. Now if we—"

Lee threw down a piece of the Semtex. It hit the ground and rolled over to Jim. Jim picked it up, examined it, then looked at Lee like he was wondering why this yokel was throwing Play-Doh at him.

"That's Semtex plastic explosive," Lee said. "I got it planted all over this building." Lee took the detonator out of his pocket and held it up so Jim and the others could see it.

After he saw the detonator, Jim carefully set down the piece of Semtex. "Well, that is a horse of a different color," he said as calmly as he could. "Everybody, be cool."

Chuck was struggling to untie himself from Hungry Jack the zombie. Whichever of these nutjobs had tied the knot had done a damn good job of it. Chuck finally gave up and hacked off Jack's forearm with the machete.

Bloody and sweaty, with a zombie's severed forearm hanging from the wrist of his right hand, Chuck got to his feet and surveyed the crowd. He spotted Blondie, still wearing his poncho. Like all of the other Eaters in the room, she was looking up at Lee with her hands in the air. Chuck walked over to the woman and took his poncho from her. He looked at her exposed breasts. "You're no Dina Meyer," he said.

The Girl grabbed Chuck by the arm. The two began backing out of the room, keeping an eye on the Eaters. The Girl had the pistol Chuck had given her aimed at the Eaters. Chuck was holding the machete like he was ready for a swordfight. "Where to now?" he asked the Girl.

"Not sure," the Girl said. "Haven't thought that far ahead."

"Did you happen to see my horse anywhere?"

"Yeah," the Girl said. She pointed in the direction opposite of the one they were walking in. "He's tied up outside."

"Damn it," Chuck said through gritted teeth.

Lee made his way down from the catwalk and joined Chuck and the Girl. The Girl walked out a door and left the big room. Chuck followed. He waved at the crowd with the machete. "Later, bitches."

Finally, Lee left the room. He closed the door on his way out.

The Zombie Eaters weren't sure what to think. A few mumbled conversations started up. People began lowering their hands.

"Listen up," Jim said. This got most everybody's attention. "I need three things. First . . . morphine, 'cause this gunshot wound hurts like a son of a bitch. Seriously. Second . . . a couple of y'all search the building for plastic explosives so we don't, you know, explode."

The Eaters looked at each other, then at Jim. Larry asked Jim, "And?"

"And what?" Jim asked.

"You said you need three things," Larry said. "What's the third thing?"

Jim sighed. "That'd be somebody to go chase those assholes, they're getting away." Jim shook his head. "Kind of thought that went without saying."

After a few seconds, several of the Eaters had an "oh yeah" moment and ran over to the door. Larry tried to open it, but it wouldn't budge. Larry explained the situation to Jim. "Door won't open. I think they blocked it."

Jim's annoyance at Larry was trending toward anger. "Well, damn it, Larry," he said. "Maybe you ought to push harder."

Chapter 9

Sewer Escape

After making their way down a stairway, through a hallway, and down another stairway, Lee, Chuck, and the Girl found themselves in the basement of the Zombie Eaters' warehouse. "Appreciate the rescue and all," Chuck said, "but I think we're at a dead end."

The Girl noticed a manhole cover in the center of the room. "Not quite," she said. She ran over to the manhole and tried to lift the cover. It didn't budge an inch.

"Manhole covers aren't easy to throw around like they are in the movies," Chuck said. He'd learned that from the commentary track on the *Escape From New York* LaserDisc. That commentary featured the movie's director and star—John Carpenter and Kurt Russell, respectively—and was one of Chuck's favorites. It was loaded with great anecdotes about how the dystopic sci-fi classic was made, including a bit about how they used wooden manhole covers as props because real ones were way too heavy.

"Yeah," Lee said. "That thing weighs like a hundred pounds."

The Girl looked at the others, frustrated. "Well, help me!"

"And you're gonna need . . ." Lee retrieved a grappling hook from his utility belt. It was tied to a length of rope. He knelt beside the Girl and hooked the manhole cover via one of its access holes. Chuck grabbed the rope and pulled.

"You hear that?" the Girl asked. Footsteps at the top of the stairs. Apparently, the Eaters had gotten past the blocked door.

Chuck finally got the manhole cover out of the way. He and the others looked through the hole, down into darkness. Lee cracked a glow stick and dropped it down the hole to give them a little light. The Girl led the way through the manhole, down the connected access ladder, and into the sewer. Lee and Chuck followed.

At the bottom of the ladder, Chuck sniffed the sewer air. "Smells a lot better than I expected." Lee and the Girl turned on flashlights. Chuck picked up the glow stick.

The Girl was about to ask which way they should go when Lee said, "This way," and started walking. The Girl walked after him, and Chuck brought up the rear. Chuck kept looking over his shoulder—he could hear Zombie Eaters making their way down the ladder and into the sewer. They were talking loudly to each other about the terrible things they were going to do to Lee, Chuck, and the Girl when they got their hands on them.

Chuck and the Girl followed Lee around a corner as the sewer tunnel cut at a right angle. Lee raised a hand, signaling Chuck and the Girl to stop. Lee pointed his flashlight at the door ahead of him. According to the sign on the door, it led to the sewer control room. Lee put an ear to the door, listened for a moment, then stepped away from the door. He threw his AR-15 rifle to Chuck. "Hold 'em off," he said.

Chuck went back to the turn in the tunnel, took a peek around the corner. He saw Zombie Eaters with flashlights, torches, and guns coming his way. Upon seeing Chuck, the Eaters opened fire. Chuck fired a couple of haphazard rounds of his own from the AR-15, then ducked back around the corner.

Lee cracked another glow stick. He opened the sewer control room door and threw the stick inside. The stick lit up the room with eerie green light, revealing it was full of zombies. The glow stick distracted the ghouls for a moment. Lee took the opportunity to off a few of the undead with his pistol, then he closed the door again.

"You been in a lot of gunfights?" the Girl asked Chuck as the two of them took cover around the corner from all of the Zombie Eaters who were shooting at them.

"You mean today?" Chuck asked, annoyed at the Girl's question. "Yeah."

The Girl shot Chuck a dirty look. Then she stepped past Chuck and around the corner and started shooting at Eaters with her pistol. She hit a couple of her targets, but the Eaters stood their ground and returned fire. A bullet cut through her leather jacket and through her left shoulder. "Shit!" she said, dropping her pistol as she instinctively grabbed her wounded shoulder.

The Girl tried to bend down and pick up her pistol, but Chuck took hold of her collar and pulled her back behind the corner. He shot off several rifle rounds one-handed for cover fire as he stepped out around the corner just long enough to kick the pistol back to the Girl.

Back at the control room, Lee was working on the zombies. He would push the door open just far enough to get his pistol inside, fire off two or three rounds, then close the door again. It was slow and gruesome work. Lee's gun and the glove on his shooting hand were both soaked in blood. The walls of the room were splattered with brains and bits of zombie skull.

There were only two zombies left standing in the control room. Lee pushed the door open with a good hard shove. The two ghouls staggered away from the door. Lee took aim at the first one and pulled the trigger of his pistol.

Click.

Out of ammo. Instead of loading another clip into the pistol, Lee holstered the handgun and removed his combat knife from its sheath. He stabbed one zombie, then the other—both took a knife blade through an eye socket.

The sound of gunfire from the shootout was getting louder, so Lee knew the gunfight was coming his way. He called out to Chuck and the Girl. "Y'all come on!"

Hearing Lee's call, Chuck encouraged the Girl to retreat with a gentle shove but accidentally hit her injured shoulder. "Son of a bitch!" she yelled in pain as she turned to run.

"Sorry," Chuck mumbled. He followed the Girl as fast as he could while walking backwards to keep the rifle aimed at any Eaters who might catch up with them.

When Lee saw the two approach, he made his way through the control room and out the door on the other side. The Girl followed him. She stopped cold when she saw the carnage Lee had left in the room. She finally got moving again and made it through the room when Chuck caught up to her.

"Lee," the Girl said. "Can you blow up the warehouse now?" Since being shot by the Eaters, she had reconsidered her earlier opinion of not being mad enough at the gang to want to destroy its base of operations.

"No, he cannot," Chuck said. "My horse is still up there."

Something up ahead caught Chuck's eye—a shaft of moonlight coming in through the sewer tunnel roof. He sprinted ahead to investigate. He didn't find the ladder and open manhole he was hoping for. Instead, there was an iron grate—heavy, by the looks of it—and no ladder. But there were some random pieces of junk nearby, including a forty-gallon metal drum.

Chuck tossed the AR-15 rifle back to Lee and started maneuvering the drum into place beneath the grate. The Eaters were catching up, so Lee did his best to keep them at bay with the rifle.

Chuck climbed up on top of the drum. He pushed against the grate . . . yeah, it was heavy as hell, just like he figured.

The Girl looked at Lee, saw he was losing ground. "Hurry!" she shouted at Chuck. "They're right behind us!"

"You wanna come up here and push for a while?" Chuck asked.

A few seconds later, Chuck finally managed to get the grate loose, slid it out of the way. "Come on," he said.

The Girl joined Chuck on the top of the drum, after which he gave her a boost up and out of the sewer tunnel. "Hey, man!" Chuck shouted at Lee in an effort to be heard over the sound of gunfire from the militia man's rifle. "Let's get out of here!"

Lee replied with a quick thumbs-up, then fired off a few more rounds.

Chuck made his way to the surface and found himself on a city street near the edge of town. The street was deserted except for the Girl.

Lee looked up from the sewer and yelled, "Catch!" Chuck barely caught Lee's explosives detonator when Lee threw it to him. Wires connected to the detonator led back down into the sewer. Chuck wasn't sure exactly what was going on, but he was very careful not to drop the detonator. Or touch anything on the detonator that looked like a switch or a button.

After he crawled out of the sewer, Lee got to his feet as fast as he could manage and took the detonator from Chuck. "Y'all get back!" he said.

Chuck and the Girl ran away from the sewer entrance. From the sounds of the shouts and footsteps below, the Eaters were about to escape from the sewer. Lee turned away from the sewer entrance. A red light on the detonator came to life when Lee flipped the switch to arm the device. Lee pressed the large button at the center of the detonator.

BOOM.

There was a terrific explosion. Chuck and the Girl steadied themselves as the ground rumbled. A fireball shot out of the sewer and up into the night sky. Eaters below screamed in terror and pain. The rumbling trailed off and a cloud of dust drifted up out of the sewer entrance.

"That ought to slow 'em down," Lee said.

"No shit," Chuck said.

* * *

"Wait a minute," Trina said. She was in the big room at the Zombie Eaters' warehouse with Jim and a few other Eaters.

Trina was the blonde woman Chuck had unfavorably compared to Dina Meyer half an hour earlier. Jim had missed that part though, because he was distracted by all the blood pouring out of his thigh via a damn bullet hole.

Now Jim was sitting in an old metal chair with his left leg extended and propped up on another chair. A fellow Eater had cut off the left leg of his jeans and bandaged up the gunshot wound on his thigh.

Trina looked at Jim's messed up leg, then at the hypodermic syringe she was holding in her right hand. "Is morphine topical?" she asked.

Jim shot an annoyed glance at Trina. "What the hell are you talking about?"

"If it's topical, you inject it near the injury. If it's general you—"

Jim yanked the syringe from Trina's hand and jabbed the needle through the bandage and into his thigh. "If it's all right with you, Trina, I'm just gonna err on the side of caution."

"Sure, Jim."

Jim sighed with relief as he began to feel the effects of the morphine. "That's the stuff."

Clint staggered into the room. He was moving slower

than usual. His mechanic shirt and jeans were covered in dust and dirt. "They got away," he said, barely containing his anger.

"You're shitting me," Jim said.

"They got into the sewers," Clint said. "Our guys almost caught up with them. Then they dropped some more explosives, blew up the sewer tunnel."

Alice slowly walked into the room. She was in worse shape than Clint. Half her face was covered in black soot. The other half was red with blood from a nasty gash on her forehead.

Jim slowly shook his head. "I have underestimated this bitch."

Clint reached into his pocket and retrieved the letter he found after the shootout at Chuck's place. "After reading this," he said, "I got a good guess as to her next move." He threw the letter to Jim.

Jim opened the letter and scanned it quickly. Some scientist . . . captured . . . Thorsby . . . the Chief . . .

"So . . . she's trying to save this guy?" Jim asked. "From the Chief?"

Clint nodded. "Looks that way."

"We gotta head her off at the pass," Jim said. "'Cause the Chief, crazy son of a bitch that he is . . . he'll kill her sure as shit. And I wanna kill her."

* * *

After Lee reeled in his detonator wire—what was left of it, at least—and put it and the detonator in his rucksack, he looked at the Girl.

"You got shot," he said, pointing at her bloody shoulder.

The Girl nodded. "I think it's a through-and-through."

Lee turned on his flashlight and moved in to get a closer look at the Girl's wound. "Yeah. You got medical training."

The Girl flashed half a grin. "Barely. I was with a militia group for a while. I was their medic's assistant. All the same, I'd rather not sew myself up if one of y'all can handle it."

"Sure," Lee said. He handed the flashlight to Chuck. "Hold this."

Chuck obliged.

Lee reopened his backpack, took out a small medical kit, and began cleaning the wound.

"Which militia?" Chuck asked.

"Detroit Defenders."

Lee started sewing up the wound. The Girl winced when the needle pierced her skin for the first time. "Shit, that hurts," she said through gritted teeth.

Chuck reached into his back pocket and retrieved a flask. He gave it to the Girl.

"You guys are ready for about anything," she said. "Like a couple of Boy Scouts." She took a swig from the flask. Then she took another swig.

"So how'd you get here from Michigan?" Chuck asked.

"Detroit Defenders were based out of Trussville," the Girl said. "I don't know where they came up with Detroit. Something about the guy who named it being a big fan of that band Kiss."

Lee continued to stitch the Girl's wound.

"What happened to the Defenders?" Chuck asked.

"I dunno. They're probably still around. I got hooked up with them through a guy. He pissed me off and I left."

"Lemme guess," Chuck said. "Another woman?"

"Nah, he was just kind of boring."

"You left what I can only assume to be the relative safety of a large armed group because your boyfriend was boring?"

"Yeah," the Girl said. "I told you. I'm impulsive sometimes."

Chuck shook his head in disbelief. "You're suicidal

sometimes."

Lee finished with the last stitch. "That ought to do it."

"Thanks, Lee," the Girl said.

Chuck pointed the flashlight at Lee, took a good look at his face. "Wait a minute. Lee. I knew you looked familiar. It's me, Chuck. I used to run Chuck's Super Video World down in Thorsby. You used to rent all those *In Search Of. . .* bootlegs, right?"

Lee raised an eyebrow behind his amber shooting glasses, then gave a little nod. "Oh. Yeah. How you been?"

"Pretty good, all things considered. At least I was until I got tangled up with this crazy woman."

Lee looked at the Girl. "I never caught your name, ma'am."

"She'd rather not say," Chuck said. "She's all mysterious and shit."

"So I rescued you," the Girl said. "Now you gotta help me with my mission. You owe me one."

"Not really. It was your fault I got captured in the first place, remember?"

"Maybe," the Girl said.

"Maybe definitely," Chuck said. "But I'll go to Thorsby with you. Not for this mission nonsense. I need to go to my old video store and look for a LaserDisc player. Since the one at my hideout got shot to shit. Also your fault."

Lee looked at the Girl. "Mission?"

"It's a mission to save the world," she said. "Wanna come with?"

Lee didn't answer. He just removed a small plastic bag from one of the large hip pockets on his military fatigues. He opened the bag and took out a small, orange, bunny-shaped snack cracker.

The Girl's eyes widened at the sight of the cracker. "Lee. Is that a cheesy bunny cracker?"

"Yeah. Want some?"

The Girl grabbed the bag of crackers from Lee. "Yes I want some!" She took out one of the bunny crackers, examined it for a moment. Then she put it in her mouth and slowly chewed it up.

"Oh, that is so good," she said. "Where did you find cheesy bunnies?"

"Hard to come by. I've been rationing this batch out for a while now. So now what's this mission?"

"Yeah. So, there's this scientist—"

"Allegedly," Chuck said.

"Working on a vaccine for the zombie virus—"

"Allegedly," Chuck said, interrupted the Girl again.

"And he's a prisoner in Thorsby—"

"Allegedly," Chuck said.

Lee considered the Girl's brief explanation. "Is a man called the Chief involved?" he asked.

The Girl's face broke into a big smile. She shot a glance at Chuck that he could only interpret as *I told you so*. Then she looked back at Lee. "As a matter of fact, there is." She ate another orange cracker.

Lee sighed. "Damn," he said. "Thought I was done with that place. But it looks like I'm going back to Thorsby."

Chapter 10

Man of Science

"Y'all hear that?"

Lee, Chuck, and the Girl were making their way south down a busted-up sidewalk somewhere on the north side of Birmingham, Alabama. Lee stopped, listened intently. The others followed suit.

"Yeah," the Girl said. "Is that a car?"

"Muscle car, probably," Lee said. "Sounds like something with a good-size engine. Whatever it is, it's coming this direction." He looked around, pointed toward the alleyway beside the building just up ahead. "Let's duck out of the way for a minute."

Chuck and the Girl followed Lee into the alleyway. The sound of the car grew louder and louder until a 1960s-era sports car came barreling south down the street. After waiting a few seconds, Lee, Chuck, and the Girl cautiously exited the alleyway.

"This road's a little busy for my taste," Lee said. "We need to get out of town. Stick to the woods and back roads for a while."

The Girl reached into her bag and retrieved the pistol Chuck had given her. "Nah," she said. "Anybody messes with us, we can just shoot 'em."

She pointed her gun at an imaginary agressor and pretended to pull the trigger. "Bang."

Lee shook his head. "Problem with that plan," he said, "you start shooting, making all that racket, you might get the attention of somebody looking for a gunfight."

"Seriously," Chuck said.

Lee and Chuck resumed their southerly walk.

The Girl frowned. Then she put the gun back in her bag and followed the others.

* * *

The hum.

The hum was constant. Monotonous.

The source of the hum was a turbine. The turbine was powered by steam. The steam was created by boiling water. The water boiled because it was heated. Burning coal was the source of the heat.

But all that was going on upstairs, on the second floor of the powerhouse. The Scientist was downstairs. Below downstairs, even, in some kind of subbasement. The Scientist had never seen the turbine for himself.

Since he'd been brought to this place, the Scientist hadn't even seen the sun. He'd tried to mark time, to keep up with how many days he'd been a prisoner, but his watch had stopped working. And without the sun for reference, the days and nights ran together.

At least there was light. The one and only good thing about being a prisoner somewhere in the bowels of the Thorsby Powerhouse was the electricity. Electricity was a hard thing to come by ten years after the end of the world. The light was generated by a couple of fluorescent bulbs. Dim, flickering, yellow green in color. Not as pleasant as sunlight, but much better than nothing. Much better than the dark.

The fluorescent light was usually the Scientist's only companion. Occasionally a zombie would wander by.

Those poor undead bastards didn't last long in the powerhouse. Other than the zombies, the Chief or one of his goons might stop in to harass the Scientist.

The Scientist preferred the company of the zombies.

"Science Man!"

Speaking of bad company. That particular taunt sounded like it was coming from the Chief himself, though the Scientist couldn't tell for sure over the powerhouse's perpetual hum.

The Scientist lay on his makeshift bunk in his makeshift cell, his wrist chained to the wall via a pair of handcuffs. The Scientist lamented the fact he spent several years studying biology but not a single minute studying the craft of lockpicking.

"Science Man!" Yeah, that was the Chief. He was closer now. The Scientist didn't care. He continued to lie on the bunk, eyes closed. He would ignore the Chief for as long as he could.

"Science Man!"

The Scientist was thinking about sunlight. How if he ever saw sunlight again, it would look impossibly blue compared to the yellow-green fluorescent light that had become his constant companion.

"Sit up, Science Man!"

The Scientist opened an eye, saw the Chief was standing right outside his cell. He sat up as commanded. The Chief could be a real prick when he didn't get his way.

The Chief opened the cell door. It wasn't locked, didn't even have a lock. Just a latch. Which didn't matter since the Scientist was chained to the wall. The door wasn't good for much except keeping the occasional zombie at bay.

The Chief stepped inside the cell. He was a pretty tall guy, six-foot-two or so. He was wearing the same camo pants and jacket he always wore. And that same stupid American flag T-shirt. Sure, the Scientist wore the same thing every day, but he had an excuse.

The Chief was holding the end of a chain in his left

hand. Which was his only hand. There was a steel blade where his right hand should have been, eight inches long and, by all appearances, razor sharp.

The chain went from his hand to the floor and out of sight from there. The Scientist tried not to imagine what use the Chief might have for a long, heavy chain. Then again, it was less scary than the Chief's ever-present blade-hand.

"I have a name," the Scientist said.

The Chief paid that statement no mind. "Tell me your story again, Science Man."

The Scientist sighed. He figured he'd told this idiot the same tale twenty times by now. "I came to Thorsby to find a—"

"A cure for zombie-ism," the Chief said.

"Zombie-ism?"

"That's what they call it, right?" the Chief asked.

"Actually . . ." The Scientist started to argue but then thought better of it. "Sure. Zombie-ism."

"And you got some PhD in zombie-ism, so you're qualified to look for a cure," the Chief said.

"Before the . . . event . . . I was a research assistant in a microbiology lab," the Scientist said. "As I've told you on numerous occasions. And I'm not looking for a cure. You can't cure dead. But a vaccine—"

"Your bullshit is consistent," the Chief said. "I'll give you that."

"It's not bullshit," the Scientist said. "It's the truth. Hence the consistency."

The Chief scratched his chin with his knife-hand, his version of stroking his beard in a contemplative manner. The Scientist had noticed this was one of the Chief's favorite mannerisms. He probably figured it made him look like some kind of badass.

"So you're still blaming this mess on little green men?" the Chief asked.

"I can't speak to any men," the Scientist said. "But my theory, and I believe it is sound . . . my theory is that there is a complex viral organism, incredibly complex, possibly biomechanical in nature. And, yes, extraterrestrial."

The Scientist had to stop his explanation for a moment to let the Chief get in a derisive chuckle.

"And this organism, it commandeers a human body, specifically the digestive and nervous systems," the Scientist said. "In the process, it kills the person, or at least renders him or her—"

The Chief had heard enough. "The federal government is to blame for zombie-ism and the destruction of this great nation. And you," he said, pointing at the Scientist with his knife-hand, "are a spy working for that same federal government."

The Scientist realized he had his hands up. It was an almost instinctive gesture when a weapon was pointed at him. Especially when the sanity of the person pointing the weapon was in question.

"I hate to interrupt your paranoid fantasy, Chief, but the United States federal government has gone the way of the T. Rex and the passenger pigeon."

The Chief raised an eyebrow beneath his ratty old camo hunting cap. Then he gave the chain he was holding a good tug. Somewhere outside the cell, something groaned in pain. A zombie? The Scientist wasn't sure what was happening, but he didn't like it. The Chief continued reeling in the chain. It was taught—there was something offering resistance on the other end.

Finally, the Chief reached the end of the chain. It was shackled to a zombie's neck. The zombie staggered into the cell, fell to its knees, and let out a pathetic moan. It looked at the Chief with its dead, milky eyes.

The Scientist backed away as far as his bonds would allow.

"I ain't no science man like you," the Chief said. "But I figured out how to cure a zombie a long time ago."

The Chief dropped the chain. His left hand free, he took the revolver from the waistband of his pants and shot the zombie point-blank in the head.

Blood and bits of brain and skull splattered on the Scientist.

The zombie fell to the floor.

The Chief pointed at the felled zombie with the still smoking gun. He smirked. Apparently he was amused with himself. "Looks cured to me," the Chief said. "What you think?"

Chapter 11

Back Roads

"Lee, I swear, you are the man," the Girl said. She was enjoying a hot dog. Well, there wasn't a bun or anything, but it was a frankfurter, and it was still hot from when Lee cooked it up over a quick campfire. "Where do you find all this stuff?"

"Just gotta know where to look," Lee said. The embers of the campfire were covered in dirt a half-mile behind him. He was now walking south through the woods adjacent to Highway 31. Chuck and the Girl followed him.

"Where does he keep it all is what I'm wondering," Chuck said, mostly to himself.

"Think we should have eaten them cold, though?" the Girl asked. "I mean, our campfire . . . it's out now, but did it send zombies in our direction?"

"No," Lee said. Actually, with his thick southern drawl, it sounded more like "naw."

"At night, zombies just like artificial light, like flashlights and whatnot. They keep away from firelight. They know it's dangerous. Some primal instinct, I guess."

"Hmm," the Girl said. "Kind of makes you think, doesn't it?"

Chuck rolled his eyes. "Nope."

Lee looked over his shoulder at Chuck, then at the Girl. "He always like that?"

"I just know where this conversation is going," Chuck said. "I heard it a hundred times back when this all started, and before that I'd already seen it in every zombie movie ever made. It's the 'what does this all mean' conversation. How do zombies reflect on us as a society? To save time, let me skip to the end for you. They don't. Zombies don't mean shit. They are dead sacks of meat that a virus or whatever has somehow jumpstarted, and that's it. End of story."

"That's what we tell ourselves," the Girl said. "We act like the zombies are these alien creatures, but maybe they're just us reduced to our most base, animal level."

"It's like I'm not even here," Chuck said.

"And you could say, well, it's the fact that they're dead and diseased or whatever," the Girl said, "but then you look at how people still living reacted to what's happening, how quickly everything fell apart and . . . I don't know. My dad, he was kind of a survivalist type before any of this happened. He used to say people weren't meant to live as the civilized creatures we pretend to be, so he wanted to be ready when it all fell apart."

Lee chuckled. "I knew a guy like that once, too."

"I always thought he was eccentric," the Girl said. "But maybe he was right."

"Based on what?" Chuck asked. "Those Zombie Eater assholes?"

"They aren't the only ones who went off the deep end when things went bad," the Girl said. "Back when I was with the Defenders, we'd get reports over shortwave from all over. Like, there was this group of skinhead types up in Virginia that thought God sent the zombies to wipe out all the non-whites in America, so they started rounding up zombies, putting them in trucks so they could drive them into urban centers and places with large ethnic populations."

Lee shook his head. "Terrible."

"Of course, it didn't work because most of them got eaten trying to round up the zombies," the Girl said. "I mean, they were skinheads, they weren't very smart. Then there was another group up in Oregon, extreme environmentalists, and they decided the zombies were Mother Earth's way of retaliating against people for all the damage we'd done to her. They killed themselves so they could become zombies, too, and fight for Gaia. More than two hundred people."

"Yeah," Lee said. "That one I heard about. I've seen stuff like that myself. Over in Georgia. People there, they're whining and fighting with each other over trivial nonsense. So much so you wouldn't even know there were still zombies around."

"So what does that prove?" Chuck asked. "That some people handle apocalyptic situations badly? No shit. That doesn't negate hundreds of years of human civilization. For every group of nuts you can come up with, I can counter with *The 400 Blows* or *Solaris* or *The Thing*."

Lee turned to shoot Chuck a confused look. The Girl didn't seem to know what Chuck was talking about either.

"Or the Sistine Chapel," Chuck said. "Or all the art in the Louvre."

"Much as I hate to do it," Lee said, "I'm gonna agree with Chuck on this one. World gets turned upside down, and people . . . people get desperate, looking for some way to make sense of it. Some of 'em are bound to fixate on the wrong things. Especially if they were troubled to begin with."

* * *

Bob wasn't too worried about the clean-cut guy, Jim. Jim seemed reasonable, and he'd wandered off, looking through Bob's considerable collection of merchandise.

Bob was worried about the dude with the handlebar mustache and the bad teeth, Clint. Clint did not seem reasonable. In fact, Bob was pretty sure Clint was a psychopath.

Clint was standing behind Bob, asking questions about Bob's customers. Bob wasn't eager to answer these questions—his customers trusted him, trusted that he was discreet, and if he betrayed that trust, those customers would take their business elsewhere. But Clint had just cut off the ring finger of Bob's left hand with a straight razor. Bob considered himself a pretty tough hombre, but he knew he wasn't tough enough to give up many more fingers. And what if Clint decided to use that razor to cut Bob's throat? The trust of his customers wouldn't be worth much to a dead Trader Bob.

"So you gonna tell me about the bitch and the Chief and his powerhouse?" Clint asked in that molasses southern drawl of his. "Or am I gonna cut off another one of your fingers?"

* * *

On the drive up to Tarant City, Iceman had planned on getting some sleep later. He'd looked forward to it, in fact. But here he was on the way back to Thorsby not sleeping, even though Clutch was driving now. And the windows were up and the radio wasn't too loud.

It was probably all the crystal meth that Iceman had smoked earlier in the evening that had him wired at this point. And since he wasn't driving and wasn't sleeping and didn't have much of anything to do in the passenger seat of the white Ford F-150 truck, he decided to smoke some more.

The flame from Iceman's butane lighter heated the crystal in the glass pipe, and Iceman inhaled deeply. When he exhaled, he sang a little song in time with the rock song playing on the radio. "Crank, crank, cra-cra-ank. Crank, crank, cra-crank."

In the driver's seat, Clutch rubbed his eyes with his left hand. He kept his right hand on the wheel. "Son of a bitch," he said. "I'm sick of this road."

"Then get on another road," Iceman said.

"I'm sick of all these roads," Clutch said.

"Yeah. Me, too," Iceman said. "But I love this crank."

Iceman looked ahead. He could make out a figure, slowly walking right down the middle of the road, on a collision course with the truck.

"Hey, man, watch out for that—"

Clutch didn't let him finish. "I'm sick of all these zombies, too."

Instead of slowing down or swerving to avoid the ghoul in the middle of the road, Clutch pressed down on the accelerator and aimed the truck straight for the undead thing.

Th-thunk.

The truck did a little double hop when its front wheels and rear wheels ran over the zombie in quick succession. Kind of like hitting a speed bump in a Wal-Mart parking lot.

"What you gonna do?" Iceman asked. "All dark out here, and zombies like the truck headlights."

Out of nowhere, another zombie was in the road ahead. *Whomp.* After the F-150 hit this one, it slid across the hood, up the windshield, and over the cab of the truck. Clutch turned on the wipers to clean off the trail of blood and dirt and shit the thing left on the windshield.

Iceman looked back into the bed of the truck to make sure the roadkill zombie hadn't landed in there. But it was dark back there, and he couldn't make out much through the truck cab's tinted rear window. Oh well. The bed was mostly full of whatever cargo they had picked up in Tarant City, so there wasn't much room for a zombie back there anyway.

By the time Iceman turned back around to look at

the road ahead, the truck was up on yet another zombie. *Th-thunk*. The truck hopped again when it ran over the ghoul. The cab shook so much that Iceman dropped his meth pipe.

"Shit, man," Iceman said. "Zombie road out here tonight." He lit his Bic and bent down, head between his legs, to look for his pipe on the truck cab floorboard. When he spotted the pipe, he noticed the truck was slowing down. He grabbed the pipe, sat back up and looked at Clutch.

"Why you slowing down?"

Clutch didn't answer, didn't even look at Iceman. He just stared straight forward. He pressed down on the brake and the truck came to a stop.

Iceman turned to see what Clutch was staring at. He almost dropped his pipe again when he saw all the zombies. More than he'd ever seen in one place, more than he could count. The road ahead was crowded with zombies as far as the eye could see.

Iceman punched Clutch on the arm. "Man, why'd you stop? Run over them damn things."

Clutch kept staring ahead, slowly shaking his head. "Shit no. Too many. Be like driving into a brick wall."

Then Clutch threw the truck into reverse and hit the gas. He turned to look behind the truck and hit the brakes again.

More zombies. The truck was surrounded. Iceman looked out the passenger-side window. The woods went right up to the edge of this stretch of road. Maybe he could make a run—

Smack. A zombie's hand feebly slapped the window. Iceman scooted away from the door with a start.

"Damn it, man!" Clutch said. He reached across and locked Iceman's door.

"Sorry!" Iceman said.

There were so many zombies trying to get into the truck, the vehicle was shaking and swaying. The zombies were crawling over each other. Their moans and groans drowned out the music from the truck's radio.

Since he didn't have anything better to do, Iceman nervously put his meth pipe to his lips. He lit the pipe, inhaled deeply. Closed his eyes.

"You hear somebody out there?" Clutch asked.

Iceman opened his eyes. Listened. Yeah, Clutch was right. Somewhere outside, on the other side of all the damn zombies, somebody shouted, "Turn off your headlights!"

"Yeah," Iceman said. "He said turn off the headlights." Iceman thought about it. That sounded like the best idea he'd heard all damn day. "Yeah! Turn off the headlights! Do it!"

Clutch flipped the switch, killed the headlights. Outside, the zombies continued to moan and groan and try to get into the truck.

"Turn off the engine, too," Iceman said. "And take your foot off the brake."

The diesel engine rattled to a stop. The truck was silent. And dark. No headlights, no interior lights, and most of the moonlight was blocked by all the damn zombies that were pressed up against the truck windows and windshield.

Clutch and Iceman sat there in the dark for what seemed like forever, just listening to the zombie noises. But then the noises got quieter, just for a second or two. When the zombies started moaning and groaning again, they also started staggering away from the truck. When enough moved clear of Iceman's window, he figured out why the zombies were moving on. There was a spotlight somewhere out in the woods, bright as hell. The zombies obviously preferred the light to the dark truck.

After watching the last few zombies make their way into the woods, Clutch started to crank the truck but stopped when he saw the road ahead was blocked. Not by zombies, but by some asshole in a poncho with an AR-15 rifle.

The Girl tapped on the Ford F-150's passenger-side window with the barrel of her revolver. She was smiling. The hastily-assembled plan to hijack the pickup truck was going pretty well so far, mainly thanks to Lee's seemingly magical backpack. When the Girl and her companions had come upon the truck and all the zombies, Lee reached into his bag and produced a small spotlight with a mostly-charged battery and said, "This might be useful."

With the zombies distracted by said spotlight, all that was left to do was to get these two goons out of the way. "Roll down your windows," the Girl said.

While the men in the truck were rolling down the windows, Chuck walked over to the driver-side door. The Girl tapped the guy in the passenger seat on the shoulder with the barrel of her pistol. "Hands on the dashboard." She looked at the driver. "Both of you."

The two men in the truck reluctantly complied.

"Did you just save us from those zombies?" the driver asked.

"Lee did most of the work," the Girl said. "But yeah."

"And now you're stealing our truck," the driver said.

Chuck reached in and took the truck keys from the ignition. "Such is the complex morality of life in a post-apocalyptic wasteland."

The Girl raised an eyebrow. "I don't know if I'd call all this a wasteland. More of a dystopia."

"You think?" Chuck asked.

The driver cleared his throat, interrupting the semantics debate. "Since you did save us from a bunch of zombies," he said, "I'm gonna give you some friendly advice. Let us be on our way, and you can carjack the next vehicle comes this way."

Lee cautiously made his way out of the woods. Seeing the situation was under control, he walked up behind the Girl.

"Why would we want to do that?" the Girl asked the driver.

"Missy," he said, "we work for the Chief of Thorsby. You steal this truck, you're stealing from the Chief. And he's been known to hold a grudge over such transgressions."

"Let me give you some friendly advice," the Girl said. "Tell us everything you know about the whereabouts of the Chief and the Scientist, and Lee here won't torture you."

Lee shook his head. "I ain't torturing nobody. Information gained from torture is generally unreliable."

The Girl frowned, glared at Chuck.

"Don't look at me," Chuck said.

The driver opened his door, exited the truck, and walked around to the front of the truck.

"Go on," the driver said. "Take the truck. As for information, the Chief's at the powerhouse. He's always at the powerhouse, everybody knows that. And when you find him, you're gonna get your asses handed to you. So y'all have fun. Come on, Iceman."

After he collected his butane lighter and glass meth pipe, Iceman exited the truck and caught up with the driver. As the two walked away, the driver saluted Lee, Chuck, and the Girl with a middle finger.

Chapter 12

King of the Pirate Airwaves

The Scientist sat on the edge of his makeshift bunk in his makeshift cell. He was still shaken from his encounter with the Chief. At least he was in better shape than the zombie lying motionless on the floor, its brains splattered on the cell wall.

"Who's your friend?" the woman at the cell door asked. The Scientist was startled. He hadn't heard her approach over the roaring hum of the powerhouse.

"Some poor zombie," the Scientist said. "And those are its brains on the wall there. Courtesy of the Chief." The Scientist had no idea who this woman was, but here he was making small talk with her. It had been so long since he'd had a conversation with a sane human being, he'd almost forgotten what it was like.

Assuming that this woman was sane. But the Scientist was happy to do that. The tone of her voice was calm, friendly. And her eyes were sad, but they were not crazy.

"The Chief," the woman said. "He's got you slated for execution."

The Scientist gave a resigned nod. "Yeah."

"Why?"

"He thinks I'm a spy working for the federal government," the Scientist said. "That's what he claims, at least. Could be he's just a homicidal asshole."

The woman offered an ironic grin. It wasn't much, but it was enough to get the Scientist to almost smile himself. Then he noticed the woman's arms, exposed by her short-sleeved shirt. They were covered with scars.

"Your arms," the Scientist said. "The scars. What happened?"

The woman offered another grin, this one sheepish. "Oh, you know. Old war wounds. Mostly zombie bites."

The Scientist's eyes grew wide. "You're immune?"

"Apparently."

"That's amazing," the Scientist said. "Do you have any idea why?"

The woman sighed. "I was the unwilling subject of some experiments."

"Who performed these experiments?"

It took a few seconds for the woman to answer. "They weren't local," she finally said.

"Like Atlanta?" the Scientist asked. "Or DC?"

"Like less local than that," the woman said. She pointed a finger toward the ceiling. "Like from another planet."

The Scientist's eyes widened. "Then my theory is correct. The zombie virus, it's extraterrestrial."

"Maybe," the woman said. Her next few words came out slowly, like she was doubting herself. "It's been so long. Since the experiments."

"The key to a vaccine," the Scientist said. "It could be inside you. We should—"

The woman cut him off. "You should leave."

"Yeah. I should. But . . ." The Scientist pulled on the handcuffs that bound him to the short length of chain that was itself bound to the wall of his makeshift prison cell thanks to a large bolt.

The woman looked both ways down the hallway outside the cell to make sure no one else was around. She stepped into the cell and took the Scientist's unbound hand in her hands.

"Good luck," the woman said. Then she left the cell and disappeared down the hall.

The Scientist sat on the edge of his makeshift bunk for a while, thinking about the woman and her scars and her story about alien experimentation. Finally, he opened his hand and looked at the key the woman had given him.

* * *

Over the dreamy-sounding intro to a psychedelic rock song, the disc jockey said, "Hope everybody out there is having a good Wednesday night. Or at least isn't being eaten alive by an undead ghoul. Anyway, here's some more music for the wasteland, courtesy of your old pal DJ Dan."

Lee was at the wheel of the hijacked white Ford F-150 pickup truck. Chuck was in the passenger seat, the Girl was in the center of the backseat, and all three were listening to 94.7 FM on the truck's Blaupunkt radio receiver. The three were traveling south on I-65 and had just passed Exit 234.

"See," Chuck said. He looked back at the Girl. "DJ Dan says it's a wasteland."

The Girl leaned forward into the space between the driver and passenger seats. "You guys know anything about DJ Dan?"

"I don't listen to him much," Lee said. "I'm more of a country and western fan."

"Where do you think he gets the electricity to run his radio station?" the Girl asked. "He couldn't be doing that with a generator, could he?"

"Not likely," Lee said, "considering his broadcasting range."

"So maybe he's getting electricity from Chief's powerhouse somehow," the Girl said.

Lee considered the Girl's theory for a moment, then he reached into his pocket for a map and handed it to the Girl. She switched on her flashlight to get a better look at the map.

Lee glanced away from the road long enough to point at a marker on the map. "Closest radio tower to Thorsby I know about," he said, "is right there."

* * *

"So we're just knocking on the front door?" Chuck asked. The question was rhetorical, as, yes, that's exactly what they were doing. Or what the Girl was doing, at least. She was knocking on the door of the building that was the home to DJ Dan's radio station. That was the assumption, based on the tall broadcast tower right next to the building and the loud music blaring from inside.

The Girl's first knocks went unanswered. Maybe Dan couldn't hear over the music. She knocked again, louder. The music inside grew quieter and someone shouted, "Hold on!" The Girl looked at Chuck and smiled.

Whoever was inside reached the door. The Girl waited while he unlocked what sounded like several deadbolts. Finally, the door cracked open and a man wearing a knit cap and horn-rimmed glasses peeked out. "You guys aren't going to shoot me or anything?"

That wasn't the greeting the Girl expected. "No?" she said.

The door opened a bit more. Not all the way, as there were still a couple of security chains in place. The man took a look at Lee and Chuck. Then he took another look at the Girl and closed the door.

The Girl was confused. She looked back at Lee and Chuck. Lee shrugged. Chuck shook his head. The Girl was about to knock on the door again when it swung back open. The man handed the Girl three T-shirts and a stack of autographed photos. DAN CLUB was printed on the front of the shirts, KING OF THE PIRATE AIR-WAVES on the back. The eight-by-ten-inch photos were all signed with a variant of *Your pal, DJ Dan*.

Dan closed the door. The Girl could hear him locking all the deadbolts again. "Wait!" she said. "We didn't come here for autographs!"

Inside, Dan let out an annoyed sigh. Then he unlocked the deadbolts and cracked the door open again. "Then why did—"

"Where do you get the electricity for your radio station?" the Girl asked.

Dan took a step back, eyed the Girl suspiciously. "Aw hell. Did the Chief send you guys?"

"No," the Girl said. Dan relaxed a bit at that. "But that's kind of why we're here. Can you tell us anything about the Thorsby Powerhouse?"

Dan smiled. "I can tell you all kinds of shit about the Thorsby Powerhouse. But what's in it for me?"

The Girl narrowed her eyes. "What?"

"Pay to play, kid," Dan said.

"You can't be serious," the Girl said.

Chuck was already walking back to the truck. "Come on. Let's get out of here."

"No, Chuck," the Girl said. "Wait." She turned her attention back to Dan. "How about some new music?"

Dan chuckled. "What, you gonna sing me some a cappella new folk bullshit?"

The Girl took the Lonely Rats cassette tape out of her pocket, held it up so Dan could see it. "No," she said. "I'm talking about an honest-to-goodness new rock song. Drums, guitar, the whole nine yards."

* * *

DJ Dan invited Lee, Chuck, and the Girl inside and back to his broadcast studio. He pulled the needle off the record that was playing mid-song and spoke into his microphone. "All right, rock and rollers, I just got a special delivery of some new music from . . ." He looked back at the Girl. "What's your name, kid?"

Chuck shook his head. "Don't ask."

"Well," Dan said, "sombebody just dropped off a cassette tape from a band called Lonely Rats. Let's see if it's any good."

Dan popped the cassette into the tape deck, hit the play button, and cranked the volume on the in-studio monitor speakers. The song, titled "Evidence" according to the hand-written label on the cassette tape, blared throughout the room.

Dan nodded his head, somewhat in time with the music. "These guys, they're working on an album?" he asked. He had to talk loudly, yell almost, to make himself heard over the music.

"A double album, technically," the Girl said.

The song's chorus kicked in. Dan listened to a couple of bars, then he abruptly left the room. Chuck and the Girl exchanged confused glances. Lee looked over his shoulder to make sure Dan was still gone, then told Chuck and the Girl, "I don't think DJ Dan's glasses are real."

Dan returned with a Sharpie and one of the THREAT LEVEL BLACK flyers. When Dan sat down at his desk next to the mixing board, the Girl took a closer look at his glasses. Yep. Lee was right—Dan's horn-rimmed glasses didn't have any lenses. Lee looked at the Girl and pointed at his own eyes with the index and middle fingers of his right hand and shook his head. The Girl got the message: *See, what did I tell you?* The Girl grinned back at Lee. Post-apocalyptic hipsters. And she thought she'd seen everything.

Dan reached over to the mixing board and brought down the volume of the music a bit. He turned over the flyer to the blank side and started drawing a crude map with the Sharpie. "Security at the powerhouse is actually pretty slack. I mean, most everybody working there is tweaked up on meth and packing heat, but there aren't many dedicated security guards."

Dan pointed to an area of the map and marked it with an X.

"This is the main entrance," Dan said. "Probably a guard there."

Dan drew another X.

"And over to the left . . . is the watchtower. There'll be a sniper up top with a spotlight."

Dan drew an arrow.

"However . . . there's an entrance back here. And they usually don't bother guarding it."

"Why don't they just lock it?" Lee asked.

"Door's old and busted up, won't close," Dan said. "I mean, they could have fixed it by now, but that's where I'd start. Go in there, take the stairs all the way down, that's where they keep people locked up. Where I did my stint, at least."

The Girl crossed her arms and smiled a self-satisfied smile. "This is gonna be easier than I thought."

"Oh yeah," Chuck said. "Walk in the park." Based on his tone, he didn't think it would be a walk in the park at all.

"It's not Alcatraz," Dan said. "Just be cool. Act like you're supposed to be there. Likely as not, you can get in and out before anybody even notices."

Chapter 13

Savage Times

While it was most likely true that Clint was a psychopath, Jim had to admit that his plan was a good one. This plan in particular—Jim knew that Clint had made plenty of terrible plans in the past.

Jim and Clint had found out from Trader Bob that the Thorsby Powerhouse was not particularly well guarded. But if even one of the Chief's goons saw even one Zombie Eater anywhere near the powerhouse, he'd sound some alarm, and then Jim and Clint would have a whole bunch of goons to deal with. If, however, that goon were to see a zombie or three approaching, he probably wouldn't give it much thought. Said goon would probably just shoot the zombies in their ugly faces and go about his business.

So Jim had stuffed three ghouls into the trunk of his '67 Camaro before him and Lee left the Eaters' warehouse. That car had a decent-size trunk, but three zombies made for a damn tight fit. The zombies were not pleased with the travel accommodations, but considering their hands and legs were bound and their heads were covered with burlap sacks, there wasn't really jack or shit the zombies could do about it.

The undead trunk passengers complained all the way from the Eaters' warehouse to Trader Bob's to the Thorsby Powerhouse. Thank goodness for DJ Dan and his pirate radio station. Dan's shit was getting tired as far as Jim was concerned, but it was certainly preferable to zombie moans and groans. What Jim really needed to do was fix the Camaro's eight-track tape player, but that was a job for another day.

Jim let the three zombies loose on the other side of the hill situated about two hundred feet north of the powerhouse. He didn't even have to encourage them to walk toward the powerhouse—they wanted to go that way because of the electric lights outside the power-house and the hum of the generator turbine.

The sniper in the watchtower caught sight of the three zombies at about one hundred feet. He called it in to the Chief and the guard at the front entrance of the powerhouse and anybody else who might have been listening to the sniper's walkie talkie channel.

While the sniper was distracted with the zombies, picking them off with his rifle in no particular hurry, Clint made his way up the stairs to the top of the watch-tower. Right after the sniper called in an "all clear" on the walkie, Clint came up behind him and slit his throat with a straight razor. That was pretty much enough to do in the poor son of a bitch, but Clint threw him off the watchtower to the ground below for good measure.

The guard at the front of the powerhouse thought he heard something but couldn't say for sure over the noise from the powerhouse. So he put down his paperback copy of *At the Earth's Core* and went over to the base of the watchtower to investigate. Jim was waiting to ambush him.

The guard seemed pretty scared, so Jim decided to let the guy live. That'd be easier than shooting the guy and maybe drawing unwanted attention from the Chief and his goons. Jim took the guard's walkie and pistol.

"Start running that way," Jim said, pointing to the hill

north of the powerhouse. "Fast. You run fast enough, I might not shoot you in the back."

The guard ran like hell.

❁ ❁ ❁

The recently hijacked white Ford F-150 drove past the THORSBY: 3 MILES sign Chuck had avoided the day before. Looking farther down the road, Lee, Chuck, and the Girl could see faint city lights.

Chuck was in the middle of a story. "And then the cab driver says, 'I thought you were dead.' And he's like 'I am if I don't find the big man.' And the cab driver lights up a Molotov cocktail and throws it out his sunroof. Because, sure, his cab has a sunroof. And it's all like 'boom.' Wait, I think I skipped a part. Where he thought he found the big guy, but it was just an old crazy guy. As opposed to the younger crazy guys popping out of the—"

Chuck interrupted himself. "Hey, we're not just hitting Main Street, driving straight into town?"

"Naw," Lee said. "You know Collins Chapel Road?"

Chuck nodded. "Good idea."

"So . . ." the Girl said.

"So?" Chuck asked.

"You were telling the story about—"

"Oh yeah," Chuck said. "The cab driver. Lights up a Molotov cocktail. Boom."

❁ ❁ ❁

After taking care of the minuscule security staff, Jim and Clint didn't have much trouble making their way into the powerhouse and down to the detention area in the subbasement. But Jim wasn't happy with what he found there.

"I'm counting one dead zombie and zero scientists," Jim said.

Clint scowled. "Yeah."

"Clint, I don't think there is a sufficient cuss word to express how mad I am at this moment. How in the hell did she get down here and break this guy out already?"

"I was thinking," Clint said, "maybe the Chief jumped the gun and executed this fella early, and the bitch don't know that, so she's still en route. We sit tight a while, she'll walk right through that door."

"That's what you were thinking?" Jim asked.

Clint smiled his disgusting smile. "Yeah."

"And who's the dumb bastard decided it was a good idea for you to start thinking?" Jim asked. He stomped out of the cell and looked out at the empty hallway. "I swear, this day has been a straight-up shitshow."

"Oh, I dunno, Jim," Clint said. He opened his straight razor, held it up to the flickering yellow-green fluorescent light. There was still a spot of the sniper's blood on the blade. Clint carefully wiped the blade on his blue jeans.

Satisfied the blade was clean, Clint looked at Jim and smiled again. "Things just might be looking up."

* * *

The quietly buzzing lamp mounted over the back door of the Thorsby Police Station bathed the empty parking lot in a warm glow. The Girl looked out and saw a few random streetlights in the distance. She thought about how it was weird being in a town with a working electrical grid ten years after civilization had fallen apart.

"The old police station," the Girl said. "It looks different."

"This is where the Chief first set up base," Lee said. "He put up the fence and stuff. Hey, wait a minute, how did you . . ."

Lee trailed off without finishing his question. "How did I what?" the Girl asked.

Chuck interrupted before Lee could answer. He'd

been looking at Lee's map and the surrounding area, trying to get his bearings. "OK," Chuck said. "This'll work. If you two get back on the road and drive another couple of miles that way, you'll end up in the woods behind the powerhouse."

Chuck showed Lee the road on the map. "You should be able to sneak in on foot from there."

Lee took a bite of jerky and looked at the map. "Sounds like a plan."

The Girl's eyes narrowed. "Wait. What do you mean 'you two'? Where are you going?"

"About a mile that way," Chuck said, pointing toward the front of the police station. "Which kind of sucks, because I'll have to go straight through the middle of town to get to my old video store."

"You were serious about that?" the Girl asked. "You're going after that stupid videodisc player?"

"LaserDisc player," Chuck said. "Remember, I explained—"

The Girl cut him off with a hard punch to the shoulder. "I can't believe you! You're going to take off when we're so close to putting an end to all this insanity and—"

Maybe it was the punch, or maybe Chuck was just tired of the Girl's continued optimism, but he was done hearing about her mission to save the world.

"We're not close to anything," Chuck said, "except maybe another shootout with another gang of psychopaths!"

Annoyed as he was, that came out harsher than he'd planned. He dialed it back when he saw the hurt look in the Girl's eyes.

"Look," Chuck said. "Why don't you guys forget about all this action and adventure? We'll go get that LaserDisc player, head back to my place, watch a couple of movies. I'll make some popcorn. It'll be fun."

"Oh yes!" the Girl said. "We can put your stupid *28 Days Later* plan into action. We'll just watch movies and wait it out."

Lee raised an eyebrow. "28 *Days Later*? That ain't a zombie movie."

Chuck was exasperated. "I know that!"

"When bad men combine," Lee said, "the good must associate, else they will fall one by one, an unpitied sacrifice in a contemptible struggle."

"Uh . . . what?" Chuck asked.

"Waiting it out is a bad plan," the Girl said.

"Well it's better than—"

"Chuck. Me and Lee . . . we're doing this."

Chuck looked at Lee. Lee nodded in agreement with the Girl.

Chuck looked like he was about to argue some more, but he reconsidered. "All right," he said. "Nice knowing you. Thanks for the ride and everything."

Chuck started to walk away.

"Wait," the Girl said.

Chuck turned back around to face the Girl. "What?"

The Girl retrieved the pistol from her bag and handed it to Chuck. "This is yours."

Chuck scoffed. "You're about to infiltrate the powerhouse, I think you'll need that a lot more than I will."

Lee shook his head, removed the M1911 pistol from his holster, held it up so Chuck could see it. "Naw," he said. "She can use this one."

Chuck put the pistol in the waistband of his jeans. He looked at Lee and the Girl one more time, then turned and walked away.

* * *

Jim lay on the floor of the cell, bleeding to death from where Clint had slit his throat. Clint was sitting on the edge of the cell's makeshift bunk, cleaning the blade of his straight razor again and watching Jim bleed.

After he was satisfied the blade was free of blood, Clint closed the razor and put it in his back jeans pocket. Then he lit a cigarette. Jim was trying to speak but managed only a gasp or two. Finally he got some words out. "Backstabbing son of a bitch."

Clint smiled. Took another drag from his cigarette. "More of a throat cutting. But mama was a bitch. Can't argue with you there."

"Fuh . . ." Jim couldn't finish the curse. He just gasped again and spit up some blood.

Clint knelt down beside Jim. "I'm gonna guess you're hoping for an explanation before you choke to death on your own blood. So. I have observed your leadership skills during this . . . I believe you called it a 'shitshow of a day.' And in regard to those leadership skills, I have found you lacking.

"You got outsmarted at every turn by one stupid, worthless bitch. Not good, Jim. Not good at all."

Clint grabbed Jim by the chin, looked him straight in the eye. "You just don't have the capacity to lead," he said. "Not in these savage times. So I have relieved you of that burden."

Jim tried his curse again. He managed a "fuh" and a "yuh." Then there was just more blood.

Clint smiled again. It would be the last time Jim would see the bastard's rotten teeth. "You are welcome," Clint said. "And thank you for the ride. Oh. Speaking of."

Clint reached into the pocket of Jim's jeans and removed the keys to his '67 Camaro. Before he put the keys in his own pocket, Clint jingled them in Jim's face as a little taunt. This really pissed Jim off, but he was too busy dying to do much about it.

Clint stood up. "Now," he said to nobody in particular. "Let's go have a talk with this Chief."

Chapter 14

Wild Bunch

The white Ford F-150 pickup truck followed the route Chuck had suggested from the police station to the powerhouse. Along the way, a few zombies had been tempted by the truck's headlights and taillights, but Lee had pity on the ghouls and drove around them instead of running them over. The spared zombies turned to follow the truck after it passed them, even though they couldn't possibly keep up. After the truck disappeared from sight, the zombies saw the faint glow of the lights of the powerhouse in the distance, so they kept shambling in that direction.

Lee parked the truck behind the powerhouse. Way behind the powerhouse—Lee and the Girl walked about half a mile from the truck before they got a look at the large, run-down brick and glass building. But they had heard the hum of the electrical genera-tor turbine from the time they exited the truck—it got progressively louder over the course of their fifteen-minute hike.

Lee found a good vantage point in the shadow of a long deserted semitrailer rig. He managed to crouch down despite his uncooperative knee. He took a look at the powerhouse's rear entrance with his binoculars.

"What are you doing down there?" the Girl asked.

Lee looked over to see the Girl standing straight up, right out in the open. He motioned to her to duck. "Get down! You wanna be seen?"

"DJ Dan said they didn't guard this part," the Girl said.

"I'm not sure taking a disc jockey's advice on how to conduct a military op is the best plan!" Lee said in a loud whisper.

Reluctantly, the Girl knelt beside Lee. "OK. Fine. I'm down here on the ground."

Lee went back to looking through his binoculars. "It does look clear. There's that door he mentioned. Open, far as I can tell. But could be it's chained from the inside or something."

"Only one way to find out. Come on!"

Before Lee could protest, the Girl was up and running toward the powerhouse's back door.

Lee watched her for a moment, shaking his head in frustration. Then he stood up as quickly as his bad knee would allow and followed her.

After she reached the back door, the Girl waited for Lee to catch up. Lee took aim with his AR-15 rifle, pointing it at the door. The Girl was armed with Lee's Colt pistol. Lee signaled for the Girl to crouch down. She complied, looked back at Lee. He gave her a nod. With that, she pushed on the door. It swung open with a creak that was drowned out by the persistent hum of the powerhouse.

There was nothing behind the door but a dark hallway.

The Girl laughed. "We're in! Piece of cake."

At that, Lee lowered his rifle. Then he heard someone running their way. "Get behind me!" he told the Girl. As soon as she did so, he aimed his rifle into the hallway.

A man came running out the door. He was so concerned with whoever might be following him that he didn't turn his head to see Lee and the Girl until he almost ran into them. Then he raised his hands when he saw the guns pointed at him. "Please don't shoot me!"

"Quiet!" Lee said in a loud whisper. He stepped past the man to get a better look down the hallway. "You alone?"

"Yes, yes," the man said. Lee couldn't see any signs that anyone else was in the hallway.

"I'm sorry," the man said. "Please. Please. Just let me go back to my cell. Don't tell him I tried to escape."

Lee had no idea who this man was talking about. But it was pretty obvious the man was frightened. Lee glanced at the Girl. Based on the expression on her face, she was as confused as Lee.

"Escape?" the Girl asked the man. "You're a prisoner here? Not one of the Chief's men?"

"Uh . . . no," the man said. "I was a prisoner. You two . . . you aren't with the Chief?"

"No," the Girl said. "We came here to rescue a scientist who the Chief is holding hostage. A scientist who's working on a vaccine for the zombie virus."

The man slowly lowered his hands. A slight smile crept onto his face.

"Rescue?" the man said. "You found my note! Holy shit, I cannot believe that worked."

"You're the Scientist?" the Girl asked.

The Scientist nodded. Lee and the Girl looked at each other, astonished.

"Huh," Lee said. "That was easy."

The Scientist took the Girl's hand in both his hands and shook it vigorously. Then he embraced Lee in a bear hug.

"Thank you!" the Scientist said. "Thank you both so much! So which way? How do we get out of here?"

"We've got a truck about half a mile away," the Girl said. "But did you find it? The cure?" She shook her head before she corrected herself. "I mean . . . vaccine."

"No," the Scientist said. "Sorry. I mean, I barely made it into town before I was captured, so I really didn't have the opportunity . . ."

The Girl lowered her head, defeated. "So. All this. All this for nothing."

Lee gently put a hand on the Girl's shoulder. "It was always a long shot. We did find him alive though. That's something."

"Strangely enough," the Scientist said, "I did discover something during my stay here that might provide insight into a vaccine."

The Girl's eyes lit up at that. "What?"

The Scientist made a quick survey of the area to make sure the coast was still clear. "There's a woman," he said. "Inside. I don't know if she's with the Chief or a prisoner or what. But she's the person who freed me. She is apparently immune to the zombie virus. So it's possible a vaccine could be synthesized from her blood."

The Girl could barely contain her excitement. "Then we've got to find her!"

*   *   *

Probably half of the streetlights in downtown Thorsby were functioning. Not bad considering there hadn't been any organized municipal organization in Thorsby—or in any other town in America, for that matter—for the past ten years.

The downside to all the light was it made keeping to the shadows more difficult. But Chuck was doing his best. He'd been sticking to the side streets and alleys, but his old video store was on Main Street, just a block away from his current location.

As Chuck walked toward the video store, he mumbled to himself, doing a bad impersonation of the Girl. "Your plan is stupid. Your plan is so stupid. You should follow my brilliant plan and fight a whole army single-handedly."

This, he thought, was coming from a woman who'd have been dead or turned into a zombie ten minutes after she left Vulcan if he hadn't helped her. But no, he was somehow the stupid one.

Chuck reached Main Street and looked at the row of storefronts opposite him. There it was—his old store with the CHUCK'S SUPER VIDEO WORLD, TOO! sign above the door. A couple of tattered movie posters were still hanging in the broken plate glass window, one for *The Day After Tomorrow*, one for *The Hunger*.

The Day After Tomorrow was a new release in 2004 and fairly dumb, even for a disaster movie. But that was OK. Chuck didn't have a problem with dumb disaster movies, and the *Day After Tomorrow* poster was pretty good, featuring the Statue of Liberty buried beneath a frozen ocean with only the hand and torch rising above the ice.

The Hunger was a stylish vampire flick from the 80s that had finally come out on DVD in 2004. David Bowie was one of the leads in *The Hunger*, and David Bowie automatically doubled the cool factor of anything he was involved with.

Distracted by the posters, Chuck didn't pay any attention to the orange Chevy Cavalier parked half a block away from him. It didn't look any different than the other deserted cars in the area. Until the orange car's engine cranked, its headlights came on, and Chuck realized it was not deserted.

"Hey, boy!" the driver of the car shouted. "Where you headin'? You need a ride?" Then the driver laughed, loudly and menacingly.

"Shit," Chuck said to himself. He took off running for the video store.

The Cavalier's engine roared, its tires squealed, and it leapt forward toward Chuck.

Since he didn't have a better plan, Chuck drew his

revolver and fired blindly over his shoulder. The driver of the car panicked. "Shit! He's got a gun!"

The car swerved. Chuck ran past the store and ducked into the adjacent alley. Behind him, he heard the sounds of breaking glass and grinding metal as the car jumped the curb, skidded across the sidewalk, and crashed through the front door of Chuck's old video store.

Chuck peeked out of the alley, finger on the trigger of his pistol, ready to shoot again. He saw the car's engine had died. Steam was pouring from its smashed radiator. The driver and passenger were motionless. The car's radio was blaring music, a hard rockabilly groove underneath some singing about TNT and dynamite.

Chuck cautiously approached the car. The faces of both men in the car were covered with blood and glass. They were unconscious or maybe worse. Chuck reached in and removed the key from the ignition. The crash alone was bound to bring some unwanted attention to the area. No reason to leave the radio blaring.

After he pocketed the car keys, Chuck glanced around the interior of the car, noticed a few glass pipes among the empty cups and old porno mags.

"Idiots," Chuck mumbled. Sometimes it seemed like everybody in Alabama these days was either a zombie or a meth head.

Inside the store, Chuck found a lightswitch. He flipped it and smiled when the light actually came on. It had been a long time since he'd encountered a working lightswitch that wasn't wired to a noisy generator.

The store was a mess. Most of the shelves had been knocked over, and there were tapes and discs all over the floor. The place had been picked over by scavengers several times in the past decade. But not many people other than Chuck gave a shit about old movies.

Chuck made his way through the store to the area behind the checkout counter. He stepped over the old iMac he'd used to track inventory and almost stepped on the LaserDisc player he was looking for. It was beneath a sweater, his old *Dawn of the Dead* T-shirt, and three boxed sets of LaserDiscs. Chuck picked it all up and set it on the counter.

Chuck examined the LaserDisc player. Thankfully, it seemed to be in good shape. Then he looked through the LaserDisc sets. There was a collection of old *Outer Limits* TV episodes . . . nice . . . a Japanese release of *City of the Living Dead* . . . ironic . . . and the original *Star Wars* trilogy.

"I forgot I had this," Chuck said, examining the *Star Wars* set. "Widescreen, pre-Lucas meddling . . ." He turned the box over and looked at the information and imagery on the back. There were photos of Luke Skywalker, Princess Leia, and, of course, Han Solo, the famous space pirate with a heart of gold played by the great actor Harrison Ford.

Chuck wondered what old Han would do in Alabama in 2014, ten years after everything went to shit. Then he decided he didn't care. "Shut up, Han Solo," he said. After Chuck grabbed the discs, the player, and the clothes, he made his way to the front of the store.

When Chuck got outside, he set the loot on the sidewalk. He opened the Cavalier's doors and dragged the two men from the car. "Hope you guys don't mind if I borrow your car," Chuck said. "I mean, assuming I can get it to crank after y'all wrecked it."

Chuck opened the trunk. He was about to put the LaserDisc player inside when he realized the trunk was already half-filled with guns. Revolvers. Semi-automatic pistols. Hunting rifles. Assault rifles. Sniper rifles. Shotguns of the single-barreled, double-barreled, and sawed-off varieties. Uzi submachine guns which, before now, Chuck had never seen outside of old episodes of *Miami Vice*.

So many guns. And hundreds of rounds of ammo. Chuck's eyes went wide as saucers.

"Holy Sam Peckinpah's *Wild Bunch*."

* * *

In the bowels of the powerhouse, Lee, the Girl, and the Scientist were cautiously making their way down the stairs from the basement to the subbasement.

"So this isn't just some run-of-the mill virus," the Girl said. "You think it was released deliberately. By aliens. As in 'from outer space.'"

"Yes," the Scientist said.

"Crazy," the Girl said. "Extraterrestrial biological warfare. It's like *War of the Worlds* in reverse."

"Maybe," the Scientist said. "But why make this woman immune? Are there others who were also made immune? Maybe it's just an experiment. Maybe it's these aliens are childish and toying with us because they consider us a lower life form. Like a kid pulling legs off a spider."

The group reached the bottom of the stairs. Lee looked around, pointed down the hallway. "That room down there?"

"Yeah," the Scientist said. "That's the cell. But I don't think this woman was a prisoner."

Lee shrugged. He took a cheesy bunny cracker from the bag in his pocket, popped it into his mouth. "Gotta start somewhere."

When the group reached the cell, Lee and the Scientist stepped inside. The Girl kept watch outside.

"Well," the Scientist said. "This guy wasn't here before." There were two corpses lying on the floor. One was a zombie with a big bullet hole in its head. The Scientist was pointing at the other one.

Something looked familiar about the mystery corpse. Lee knelt down to get a better look. "What the . . ." Lee mumbled. Then he called out to the Girl. "Hey. Look here."

The Girl looked in from the hallway.

"It's that Zombie Eater fella that's been after you," Lee said.

"What's he doing here?" the Girl asked.

Lee got to his feet, shook his head. "I'm not liking this. We need to—"

Out of nowhere, a burly man had the Girl in a choke-hold with a gun to her head. The aggressor, a man with blond hair and a scruffy beard, moved fast for a big guy.

"Do. Not. Move."

The Scientist ignored the command and put his hands up to show he was unarmed.

Lee didn't move. He didn't need to—he already had his rifle aimed at the burly man's head.

"All right, tough guy," the burly man said. "I see that rifle you got aimed at me, and you're probably thinking you're some kind of Deadeye Dick, and you can shoot me in the face, and the little girlie here will get out of this none the worse for wear except maybe ringing ears and some of my brains on her leather jacket."

That was, in fact, pretty much exactly what Lee was thinking. He was, in fact, about to pull the trigger on his AR-15.

"You're probably right," the burly man said. "But as soon as you do that, my friend Rutger out here, he's gonna toss a grenade in that cell, and that'll be the end of all of us."

Rutger, with his slicked-back black hair and bushy beard, peeked in from outside the cell. He showed Lee the grenade in his hand, then quickly ducked back out of the cell. "You guys should listen to Rodney here," Rutger said. "Me and him both got our affairs in order, so we're ready to go right to hell today if y'all won't be reasonable."

Rodney smiled. "So how about you just slide that rifle out here, soldier man. Then you and the science dude can come on out. With your hands up, of course. Then we'll go have us a visit with the Chief."

Lee, frustrated, dropped his rifle to the floor. He gave it a kick. It slid across the floor and stopped at Rodney's feet.

Rodney stroked the Girl's cheek with the barrel of his revolver. Her eyes were stinging with angry tears.

"You, too, sweetie," Rodney said. "Drop your gun and take that pig sticker off your belt."

Chapter 15

Reckoning

With the guns of Rodney and Rutger at their backs, Lee, the Girl, and the Scientist slowly made their way up a series of staircases that took them from the powerhouse's subbasement to its basement to its ground floor. The group walked past the men who fed coal to the powerhouse's massive furnace. Finally, they walked up the staircase that led to the large generator platform some twenty feet up from the ground floor.

There were four large generator turbines on the platform, but only one was currently spinning. The other three were in various states of disrepair. A couple of the Chief's men were working on one of them, their tools scattered on the floor around them.

Smoke and steam drifted up to the platform through a large opening near the staircase. A guard rail around the opening was in place to prevent anyone from falling back to the ground floor, but it had gaps that rendered it less than effective.

With the smoke and steam, heat drifted up to the platform as well. The Girl, dressed for the cold outside, had broken into a sweat seconds after she'd reached the top of the stairs.

From the generator platform it was at least another thirty feet to the building's ceiling. A row of large windows was set near the ceiling, most of them cracked or broken. Lightning flickered in the distance—an autumn storm was brewing somewhere to the north.

"Hold them there," a man said, almost shouting to be heard over the hum of the turbine. He was lurking in the shadows on the other side of the platform, near the powerhouse's north wall.

"That's the Chief," the Scientist said, as quietly as he could. Yeah. The Girl kind of figured that was the case.

"They shot Mike out the tower," Rodney said. "Still can't find Tim, no telling what they did to him. But we caught 'em. They were trying to free the prisoner."

"How about that, Science Man," the Chief said. "I guess you're a little more important to your government friends than you let on. Just like I said."

The Girl looked at the Scientist. He shook his head, dispirited.

"Rodney," the Chief said.

"Yes, Chief?"

"It's after midnight," the Chief said. "That makes today the twentieth, right?"

Rodney thought about it, scratched his head with the barrel of his revolver. The Girl was making a hasty escape plan in the event this idiot blew his brains out. But she wouldn't be that lucky.

"I think so," Rodney said. "I get confused. Was last year a leap year?"

"Close enough," the Chief said. He gave a wave of his hand. "Take him."

Rodney and Rutger grabbed the Scientist and dragged him away from Lee and the Girl. The two guys working on the broken turbine exchanged a glance that said they didn't like where this was going, after which they hurried off down the stairs.

Rodney and Rutger stopped at one of the other inactive turbines and began chaining the Scientist to it.

"You assholes!" the Scientist said.

"Wait!" the Girl said. "We haven't shot anyone. Not here anyway. And we aren't with the government. We aren't with anybody."

"So you're just out rescuing people for fun?" the Chief asked.

"I just wanted to find out if he really found a vaccine," the Girl said.

"Ah," the Chief said. "But then . . . how'd you know to look for him here?"

"He sent a message."

"A message?" the Chief asked.

"A note," the Girl said. "In a bottle. On a rope tied around a . . . a zombie's neck."

At that, the Chief laughed loudly.

"OK," the Girl said. "I know how that sounds."

The Chief laughed some more. "It sounds delightful. Oh my. You are something. Your stories are better than the Science Man's."

Lee looked at the Girl. "This Chief's an even bigger asshole than I expected."

The Chief pointed accusingly at Lee with his knife-hand. "I don't remember giving you permission to speak, zombie."

Lee and the Girl exchanged a puzzled look.

"All right, science guy," Rutger said. "Under authority of the Chief, in the interest of protecting the sovereign community of Thorsby, I hereby—"

"And so forth and so on," Rodney said. He apparently wasn't much for ceremony.

At that, Rodney and Rutger both unloaded their revolvers into the Scientist. Twelve rounds at point-blank range. It was gruesome.

From his place in the shadows, the Chief smiled approvingly.

Lee and the Girl looked on in horror.

Rodney and Rutger, satisfied their work was done, walked back across the generator platform and down the stairs. Lee and the Girl were now alone with the Chief.

The Girl's cheeks were wet with tears. "Damn it! What is wrong with you? That man was just trying to do what he could to bring an end to this mess. He wasn't part of some conspiracy. And neither are Lee and me. We don't give a damn about you!"

"You have a kind face," the Chief said. Suddenly, his demeanor was calmer. He seemed almost reasonable. "You remind me of someone I knew a long time ago. I almost . . . I almost want to believe you."

The Chief pointed his knife-hand at Lee again. "But . . . but you brought that zombie into my powerhouse."

Again Lee and the Girl exchanged a confused look.

Lee looked back at the Chief. "What are you talking about? How many zombies you seen can carry on a conversation?"

"But I saw you die," the Chief said. He stepped out of the shadows, pointing at Lee the whole time. "With my own eyes, I saw you die!"

When the Girl finally got a look at the Chief's face, she gasped. She recognized this man. She looked at Lee and could see by the expression on his face that he too recognized the Chief.

"Keith?" Lee asked.

The Chief nodded in acknowledgement.

The Girl's eyes filled with tears again. "Dad," she said.

Keith looked like he'd just been punched in the stomach. He took an unsteady step back, almost fell through the opening to the furnace area below the generator platform. "What?"

Lee looked at Keith, then at the Girl. "What?"

"Dad. It's me. Natalie."

"Natalie?" Keith asked. "No. No. That's not possible."

Natalie wiped the tears from her eyes. She carefully took a couple of steps in Keith's direction.

"Yes, Dad," Natalie said. "It is. It's me. I didn't die in

the car wreck. Hanna, my sister Hanna, your daughter . . . she was infected, turning into a zombie."

A glimmer of recognition flashed in Keith's eyes.

"Hanna bit you," Natalie said. "You were driving, you lost control of the car, we wrecked. I thought everyone else in the car was dead or a zombie . . . I was scared, so . . . I ran away."

"Natalie," Keith said. He took a tentative step in her direction. "I had no idea."

"Why . . . how did you . . . how are you still alive?"

Keith raised his arm to show Natalie the eight-inch blade where his hand should be. "Cut out the infection before it spread. But how did you survive? Alone all this time?"

"You taught me," Natalie said. "You taught me how to survive. Remember?"

Keith smiled. He began to slowly walk in Natalie's direction. "I never thought—never imagined, not in my wildest dreams—that I'd ever see you again. I'm sorry."

Keith embraced Natalie in a hug. A tear streamed down his cheek. "I'm so sorry, Natalie."

"It's not your fault. You didn't know."

"But I do know," Keith said. He stopped hugging Natalie and backed away from her. "That's why I'm sorry."

Then Keith turned to Lee and stabbed him in the stomach with his knife-hand.

Natalie screamed in horror. "No!"

Lee, shocked, speechless, stumbled back and fell through the opening in the platform, down to the area below, near the coal furnace.

Natalie ran over to the edge of the opening, looked down at Lee. He was lying motionless on the concrete floor of the powerhouse, blood slowly pouring out of the hole in his gut.

Natalie turned to face Keith, fury in her eyes.

"Had to be done," Keith said.

"Why?"

"He was part of it, Natalie," Keith said. "He was here to destroy me and everything I've built. They can't stand that we don't need them, that we can survive on our own without them controlling us."

"'They?' Who exactly is that?"

"The federal government," Keith said. He pointed down to Lee on the floor below. "I know all about that one. Spying on me. Even before all this zombie shit started. Pretending to be my friend . . ."

Keith gave Lee an ironic salute with his knife-hand. "Not anymore."

Keith returned his attention to Natalie. "Fortunately, my new deputy told me all about you two before you arrived." Keith glanced back over to the stairs. Natalie turned to see what he was looking at.

It was Clint. He stepped off the top stair onto the generator platform. Natalie was stunned. She backed away from Keith and Clint. Not that she really had anywhere to go.

Clint smiled at her. "Hey there, little rabbit."

Natalie hated Clint, hated his smile, hated every disgusting, rotten tooth in his vile head. She looked back at Keith. "Dad. No."

"So the Chief is your old man," Clint said. "I did not see that coming."

"Dad, please," the Girl said. "Listen to me. This guy, he's not your friend. He's nuts. He's with this gang. They're all nuts. They eat zombies."

Keith walked over to stand next to Clint. "I'll trust a Zombie Eater over a government sympathizer any day of the week."

Keith put a hand on Clint's shoulder. He didn't notice Clint's scowl at being touched.

"Trust him?" Natalie asked, disgusted. "Over your friend? Over your own daughter?"

Natalie pointed an accusing finger at her father. "You have lost your shit," she said. "Utterly and completely."

"So you, too?" Keith asked. "They've turned you

against me, just like they did your mother."

"What? Mom adored you. She loved you more—"

"Agents of the federal government," the Chief said, a self-satisfied grin on his face.

Natalie shook her head. "Stop it, Dad! Just stop it!"

Clint brushed Keith's hand away from his shoulder. "I hate to interrupt this family reunion, but I've got business of my own to attend to. Chief. Been nice working with you."

With that, Clint pulled his revolver from the waistband of his jeans and shot Keith square in the chest. Keith looked at Clint in disbelief, then staggered over to Natalie and fell at her feet.

"Dad!" Natalie said. She knelt down beside her father. Blood poured from the bullet wound. He was unresponsive. Natalie knew he wouldn't last long.

Clint laughed contemptuously. "Keep it together, girl. Please. Until five minutes ago you thought your daddy was long dead. Don't get all bent out of shape about it now. You said it yourself. That guy was gone."

Natalie glared at Clint through tearful eyes. "Rot in hell, you crazy son of a bitch."

"Oh, I'm not crazy," Clint said. "I'm just making a few changes. The Chief, he was thinking too small. He had all this power. Electricity . . . actual power.

"And he had the crystal meth. Lots of people will do just about anything for some good crank.

"Forget about the Chief and his deputies and all that shit. What this place needs is a monarchy. And darlin', you are looking at the new king of Thorsby. What you say? Wanna be my queen?"

Natalie wiped the tears from her eyes. "I am going to kill you," she said. It sounded less like a threat and more like a simple statement of fact.

Clint laughed. "I'm gonna take that as a 'no.' Too bad." He aimed his pistol at Natalie. "Looks like you're all out of running, little rabbit."

A gunshot rang out. Natalie winced, then quickly

realized she had not been shot. She looked at Clint. His face was twisted in pain. His right hand—the hand that had held the revolver he was about to use to kill Natlie—was bleeding. Clint's pistol was on the platform floor at his feet.

Natalie and Clint both looked down to the main floor of the powerhouse. There was Chuck, standing near the bottom of the stairs, holding a rifle aimed at Clint. Even though he'd traded in his poncho for his old sweater and *Dawn of the Dead* T-shirt, he'd just shot the gun out of Clint's hand like a real cowboy.

Chuck didn't just have a rifle. He was armed to the teeth, with three pistols tied to his belt, two more rifles strapped to his back, and a bag full of ammo slung over his shoulder.

With a smirk on his face, Chuck looked Clint straight in the eye. "Yee haw, motherscratcher," he said.

"This clown again," Clint mumbled to himself. He dove to the platform floor before Chuck could shoot at him again. He pulled a walkie talkie from his back pocket. "Help! They've killed the Chief! Everybody get up here now!"

Chuck ran toward the stairs, stopped when he realized one of the goons working the coal furnace was shooting at him. Chuck retreated and took cover. He looked back to see more of the Chief's men flooding in from downstairs. They hadn't wasted any time answering Clint's call for help.

With Clint injured and unarmed, Natalie saw she had a brief window to finish off the miserable prick. She looked at Keith's lifeless body, saw the knife on his belt. She grabbed the knife, got to her feet. Clint saw Natalie make her move and knelt for his revolver. But Natalie was too fast. She went at him, slashed with her father's knife. Clint backed away from the pistol, but not quickly enough. Blood dripped from a fresh cut on his cheek.

Clint got to his feet, wiped the blood from his face.

Natalie risked a glance down to the powerhouse floor. From the looks of things, Chuck was in the middle of a pretty serious shootout. Chuck would never let her hear the end of it. Assuming, that is, she survived this encounter with Clint.

The self-proclaimed King of Thorsby looked at Natalie, smiled. "Nice knife." He reached into his back pocket, removed his straight razor. He opened it, showed it to Natalie. "But I got a blade of my own."

Clint adopted a fighting pose. "And I know how to use mine."

Clint lunged at Natalie. She parried his attack. Got behind him, elbowed the back of his head. That dazed Clint a little. He turned, slashed at Natalie. Missed. His failed strike left his right side exposed.

Natalie dug her knife into Clint's exposed side. He screamed in pain, fell to his knees. Clint looked up at Natalie, realized he had dropped his straight razor. He was defenseless.

Natalie kicked Clint in the chest. He fell backwards, landed flat on his back. He was dazed again when the back of his head landed hard against the concrete of the platform floor.

"I know how to use mine better, bitch," Natalie said. With that she drove her knife straight through Clint's throat. He stared at her, utterly defeated. He let out a wet, pathetic gasp.

Natalie got to her feet. She left the knife in Clint's throat. She grabbed his revolver and headed for the stairs. She had made it down three steps when a bullet whizzed by her head.

A couple of Keith's goons had started shooting at her. She ran back up the stairs, out of the line of fire. She looked down, saw Chuck.

"Hold up there!" Chuck said.

"You think?" Natalie asked, sarcastically. She looked down through the opening in the platform. Keith's men weren't expecting an attack from above. She was able to shoot a couple of them before they got wise and returned fire. Before she ducked back out of the way, she notice that Lee was gone.

Natalie stepped down the stairs far enough to spot Lee. He had managed to crawl about twenty feet from where he fell, a trail of blood behind him. He had found cover, but it wouldn't be long before Keith's men noticed him.

"Chuck!" she said. After she got his attention, she pointed at Lee. Chuck untied one of the revolvers from his belt. He got Lee's attention, then threw the weapon to him.

Lee was in bad shape, on the verge of blacking out. But the opportunity to join the gunfight gave him a boost of energy. He fired three times, and three of Keith's men fell.

Something strange was going on. There was still a lot of shooting, but the bullets didn't seem to be going in Chuck's direction. Natalie looked back down through opening in the platform to see zombies attacking Keith's men. A shitload of zombies, in fact. They must have come in through the back door after she and Lee had left it open.

Natalie ran downstairs, caught up with Chuck who had taken cover near Lee. She looked over to the front entrance, saw zombies were starting to come in through it as well.

"Get him up," she said. "We gotta get out of here."

Chuck looked up at Natalie. He didn't say anything, just shook his head.

"Naw," Lee said. "You two go on."

Natalie knelt beside Lee. "We're not leaving you," she said. "We can get you out of here."

"And what then?" Lee asked. "Run me by the hospital? I'm stabbed in the gut, my good leg is all busted up . . . I'm done for, Natalie."

Chuck looked at Natalie, a hurt look on his face. "You told him your name?" he asked.

Natalie ignored Chuck. All her attention was on Lee. "Lee. I'm sorry. I don't know what else to say. I—"

"Nothing for you to be sorry about," Lee said. "We both had our missions. Now I'm gonna finish mine."

Lee reached into his pocket, removed the last of his Semtex plastic explosive. "I'll give y'all five minutes to get clear."

Chuck got to his feet. "Take it easy, Lee."

Lee nodded, smiled. "I'll take it however I can get it."

Chuck handed Lee another pistol. Then he shot down several of the zombies coming in through the front entrance. He looked back to Natalie. "We gotta go."

Lee opened another pocket, retrieved his bag of cheesy bunny crackers. He gave the bag to Natalie. "You take these."

Natalie looked at the bag of orange crackers, then back at Lee. She smiled at him, her eyes full of gratitude and sadness.

"Y'all go on," Lee said.

Reluctantly, Natalie got to her feet. She followed Chuck as he used the rifle to clear a path through all the zombies staggering into the powerhouse through the front entrance.

Outside the powerhouse, the approaching zombies ignored Chuck and Natalie. The ghouls were more interested in all the noise and light coming from inside.

Chuck and Natalie didn't speak. They weren't sure how far they needed to go to get clear of the imminent explosion, so they just kept running. Finally they crossed a hill and ducked down on the other side of it.

They were both exhausted from their sprint. "You think it's been five minutes yet?" Natalie asked. Chuck shrugged. The two cautiously peeked back over the hill. They immediately took cover again when the powerhouse flew apart in a massive explosion. The ground rumbled. A massive fireball leapt into the sky.

For a few minutes, neither Chuck nor Natalie said

anything. They just sat there on the edge of the hill, watching the powerhouse burn. Finally, Natalie spoke. "Thanks. For coming back."

Chuck grinned. "Sure," he said. "Watching movies by yourself can get dull. It's more fun with friends."

For the first time in a long while, Natalie smiled. "You know where we can get a drink?" she asked. "I could really use a drink."

"Whiskey and some mediocre home brew OK?" Chuck asked.

"That'll work," Natalie said.

Chuck heard something behind him. He quickly turned and took aim with his rifle. A woman walked over the hill. "Wow," she said. She indicated the burning remains of the powerhouse. "So that happened."

"Lady, are you out to get shot?" Chuck asked.

"No," the woman said. "That's why I left when I heard all the gunfire."

"Are you one of my dad's . . . I mean, one of the Chief's people?" Natalie asked.

"Not really," the woman said. "He saved my life a long time ago, so I stayed around. Felt like I owed him something. But lately, he's been . . . difficult."

"Saved your life?" Natalie asked. "Were you . . . were you in a car wreck with him like ten years ago?"

"Yeah, how'd you—"

"I recognize you!" Natalie said. "You're Gail! You were in the car with us."

Natalie was putting it all together. "You were abducted by aliens . . . that means . . . you're the one the Scientist was talking about! You're immune to the zombie virus."

Gail offered a sheepish grin. "Yeah. That's me."

"I can't believe we found you," Natalie said.

Natalie turned to Chuck, excitement in her eyes. "Do you know what this means?"

"I obviously missed a lot of stuff while I was gone," Chuck said, "so no."

Chapter 16

Phase Two

The voice on the radio was singing about the stars in the night sky, and how the light we see from most of those stars is hundreds or thousands of years old. So, like it or not, we're always looking to the past. At least on starry nights.

But nobody in the white Ford F-150 was paying much attention to the radio. It was barely audible over the rumble of the big truck's diesel engine. And tonight was not a starry night. Clouds had overtaken the sky, and it had started to rain. The truck's windshield wipers moved back and forth, making a quiet *whomp-whomp* sound.

"All right . . . all right, yes," Chuck said. "Technically, you were right, and I was wrong. But we really didn't find what you were after. We just found her."

Chuck glanced over his shoulder at Gail, who was sitting in the backseat. "No offense," he said.

"The Scientist is dead," Chuck said. "So now to truly complete your mission, you'd have to find another scientist with a lab setup somewhere who could synthesize a vaccine from Gail's blood. I mean, we're a long way from a home run here."

Natalie was watching the raindrops on the outside of the passenger-side window. "If you want to be a Debbie Downer, go ahead. But after all the horrible shit that's happened today, one good thing happening gives me hope, and I'm hanging on to it."

The truck slowed to a stop. Chuck switched off the headlights and threw the transmission into neutral.

A hundred feet ahead of the truck, three zombies were slowly staggering across the road.

"What are you doing?" Natalie asked. "Just run over them."

"If it's all the same to you," Chuck said, "I've seen enough carnage for the week. Heck, for the year. So let's just give them a minute to get out of the way, and we can drive around them, and what the hell is that noise?"

At first, Natalie and Gail weren't sure what Chuck was talking about. Then they heard it, too. A pulsating hum. Eerie. It was coming from somewhere outside the truck. Maybe overhead? It was slowly getting louder.

Static interrupted the music playing on the truck's radio. Then the radio went silent. The truck's engine died. Natalie and Gail looked at Chuck, but he didn't know what was going on either. The pulsating hum continued to grow louder.

Suddenly, an intense beam of white light from overhead shone down on the zombies on the road ahead. The ghouls stopped their slow march across the road and looked up into the light.

"Oh no," Gail said. "They're back."

"Who's back?" Natalie asked.

"The aliens," Gail said.

Chuck looked up through the windshield in an attempt to get a look at whatever was overhead. "Are we getting abducted? I do not want to get probed."

"I don't think we're getting abducted," Gail said.

As suddenly as it appeared, the light from above was gone, and the strange pulsating hum of the spaceship overhead—or whatever it was—quickly faded to silence.

The truck's radio came back on. Its engine started back up.

Chuck turned the headlights back on. Out on the road ahead of the truck, the three zombies were lying motionless on the cracked and broken-up pavement.

"What just happened?" Natalie asked.

"Did they just, like, switch the zombies off?" Chuck asked.

"Is that it?" Natalie asked. "Is their experiment or whatever over?"

Gail thought about it for a moment. "You said ten years. Ten years since the car wreck. So that means ten years since this all started."

"Ten years to the day," Chuck said. "What of it?"

A hand slapped down on the hood of the car. One of the zombies had crawled to the truck and was trying to get back on its feet. Apparently, the zombies hadn't been "switched off" after all.

"Phase two," Gail said.

"Phase two?" Natalie asked. "What is phase two?"

The zombie in front of the truck had managed to get to its feet. But it didn't look like a zombie anymore, not any kind of zombie that Natalie had ever seen. Most zombies were thin, emaciated. This thing was huge. And tall—it was at least seven feet in height.

The bizarre creature's face was long, distorted. It's ears were almost comically oversized, pointed at the top. Each of the monster's long fingers were tipped with a sharp, black talon. Its rotting skin was somehow scaly and furry at the same time.

Everyone in the truck was struggling to describe the beast before them. Gail was the first one to say something out loud. "I'm guessing, maybe . . . zombie werewolves?"

Natalie could only offer a slight nod. As crazy as Gail's description sounded, it was better than anything

Natalie had come up with.

Chuck threw his hands up in defeat. "That's it. I'm done. I'm going back to my place and watching some movies. Screw these aliens."

AVAILABLE ON HOME VIDEO
FROM CREWLESS PRODUCTIONS

Hide and Creep (2004)

A MOVIE ABOUT ZOMBIES AND OTHER THREATS TO NATIONAL SECURITY.

The precursor to *For a Few Zombies More*! In the tiny town of Thorsby, Alabama, the dead begin rising from their pine boxes and feeding on the locals. A video store clerk joins forces with the police receptionist, a retired deputy, and the single G-man dispatched to the site. Together they arm themselves with whatever weapons they can find and unleash a dose of southern justice on the army of the living dead.

Interplanetary (2008)

MONSTERS AND MAYHEM, FORTY MILLION MILES FROM EARTH!

Nine men and women, employees of the Interplanetary Corporation, live and work on Mars. Their days aren't particularly interesting, much less exciting, until they are assaulted by a murderous band of strangers and a seemingly unstoppable alien creature.

FIND OUT MORE AT WWW.CREWLESS.COM